APPEARANCES

BENEATH THE SURFACE LIES THE TRUTH

MAYANK GUPTA

Contents

Acknowledgements   *v*

Prologue   *vii*

1. Into The Heart Of Campus   1

2. Clashing First Impressions   7

3. A Night Of Secrets   14

4. Mentor's Wisdom   21

5. Spirit Of Sangathan   29

6. Whispers In The Mountains   50

7. Shadows Of Affluence   59

Interlude: Anticipations

8. Fault Lines   71

9. Debate   81

10. Winds Of Change   89

11. Tangled Web Of Emotions   100

12. Amidst The Festive Frenzy   110

13. Moonlit Confessions   118

14. The Weight Of Dawn   128

15. Fractured Ties   136

16. A Dance Of Emotions   144

17. The Cost Of Silence   152

Interlude: The End Of Innocence

18. Paths Converge   165

19. New Friendships And Revelations   179

20. A Glimmer Of The Past   184

Contents

21. Unwritten Chapters   192

22. The Unspoken Farewell   199

23. A Letter To Anushka   207

Feedback Questions   211

Disclaimer   213

About The Author   215

Acknowledgements

Writing this book has been a journey of growth and inspiration, made possible by the support of remarkable individuals.

First, I want to thank my family for their unwavering love and encouragement. Special thanks to my father for always believing in me and providing me with solid support. I still remember your expression when I first told you about my book. You were filled with joy and pride. Your belief in me gave me the strength to pursue this dream and bring this story to life.

A heartfelt acknowledgement goes to **Dr. Raina Midha**, whose wisdom and guidance during my time at Amity University deeply influenced my approach to writing. Your impact is woven into every page of this book.

I am also grateful to **Dr. Tarsem Chand**, my new mentor, whose inspiration and encouragement have been invaluable in completing this work.

Lastly, to my readers, thank you for exploring the world I've created. I hope this story resonates with you.

With deepest gratitude,
Mayank Gupta

Prologue

Welcome to the world of Amity College, where the vibrant energy of youth collides with the secrets that linger just beneath the surface. Within these pages, you'll find more than just the thrill of college life; there are friendships forged in fire, romances that burn bright, and mysteries that unravel in the most unexpected ways.

As you journey alongside Arjun and his friends, you'll witness the highs and lows of love and ambition, the tension between appearances and reality, and the shadows that threaten to disrupt even the closest bonds. But be warned: not everything is as it seems. Beneath the glamorous facade lies a story filled with twists, hidden truths, and choices that will shape the futures of those who dare to face them.

Prepare yourself for a tale where every turn of the page brings new surprises and where the heart's deepest desires are often masked by the secrets we keep.

Let the mystery begin.

CHAPTER I

INTO THE HEART OF CAMPUS

Arjun Mehta stood at the entrance of Amity College, Noida, feeling like he was at the edge of something monumental. The campus stretched out before him, with 100 acres of red-brick buildings, wide pathways, and endless possibilities. His heart pounded with a mix of excitement and nervousness. He had imagined this day for years, but standing here now, it felt surreal.

Arjun (muttering to himself): "This place is massive."

He took a deep breath and stepped through the gates, immediately swept up in the energy of the campus. Groups of students flowed around him, laughing, talking, and moving with purpose. Some looked completely at ease, while others, like him, seemed a bit wide-eyed, trying to take it all in. The buzz of conversations, the thud of footsteps, and the occasional shout from a distant game filled the air.

Yash (calling out): "Hey, you look lost!"

Startled, Arjun turned to see a tall guy with messy hair and a friendly smile walking up to him.

Yash (grinning): "First day, huh?"

Arjun (nodding): "Yeah... it's a bit overwhelming."

Yash (laughing): "You're telling me! I'm Yash. Just started here, too."

Arjun (shaking hands): "Arjun. Nice to meet you. Do you know where F Block is? I'm trying to find the orientation."

Yash: "Same here! I think it's that way. Let's figure it out together."

As they started walking, Yash pointed things out, his voice brimming with excitement.

Yash: "That over there is D Block. The cafeteria's inside. Heard it's the best place for snacks between classes. And see that open space? That's H Block, basically the social hub of the campus. You'll find people hanging out there all the time."

Arjun glanced at the bustling area Yash pointed out. Students were scattered everywhere, on benches, sipping coffee and chatting in groups. The atmosphere was casual yet electric as if everyone were part of something special.

Arjun (thinking):*This place feels alive. Like it has a pulse.*

The red-brick buildings loomed around them, solid and imposing, their ivy-covered walls adding a touch of nature to the otherwise grand structures. Arjun couldn't help but feel a little overwhelmed, but at the same time, there was a growing sense of excitement in his chest.

Arjun (softly): "It's like a whole new world."

Yash (smiling): "Yeah, it kind of is. Wait until the festivals kick in; this place really lights up. I've heard the events here are legendary."

They reached F Block, a tall, imposing structure that seemed to anchor the campus. Inside, students were rehearsing dance routines in a vast, open space, their music echoing off the walls.

Yash: "Looks like they're getting ready for something big."

Arjun: "I can feel the energy everywhere... it's amazing."

They entered the auditorium, which was already packed with students. The air buzzed with anticipation. Arjun and Yash found seats near the middle of the room. As they settled in, Arjun glanced around at the hundreds of other first-year students, each one probably feeling some version of what he was feeling.

Arjun (thinking):*So many people... so many stories. We're all starting something new here. Feels like the beginning of something big.*

The college president stepped onto the stage, and a hush fell over the room. His speech was brief but impactful, speaking of the opportunities that awaited and the hard work that would be required to seize them. Every word seemed to strike a chord with Arjun. He couldn't stop thinking about the possibilities, what he could accomplish here, who he might become.

When the orientation ended, Yash turned to him with a grin.

Yash: "So, what do you think?"

Arjun (smiling): "I think this place is going to be incredible."

They stepped out of the auditorium and back into the bright afternoon sun. The campus felt even more alive now, students heading in every direction, the hum of conversations filling the air.

Yash: "You want to stick together for a bit?"

Arjun (grinning): "Actually, I think I'll explore on my own for a while."

Yash (laughing, giving Arjun a clap on the back): "Go for it, man. I'll catch you around."

Arjun set off on his own, eager to take in as much as he could. He wandered past the gym, where the clanking of weights and the rhythmic pounding of treadmills created a backdrop of intense focus. He peeked into the library, a two-story sanctuary filled with rows of books and the soft glow of laptops. Students sat in deep concentration, flipping pages or typing away, oblivious to the world around them.

Arjun (thinking): *This place feels like a city of its own... there's so much to see, so much to do. I can't wait to be part of it all.*

Eventually, he found himself by the sports fields, where volleyball, basketball, and cricket matches were in full swing. Laughter and shouts of encouragement echoed across the open space. He paused by the cricket pitch, watching as a bowler sprinted forward, delivering a fierce ball to the batsman.

Cricket Player (calling out): "Want to join us?"

Arjun (smiling and waving): "Maybe next time!"

Arjun (thinking): *Not today. Today's about soaking it all in.*

As the sun began to set, casting a golden light across the campus, Arjun made his way back to H Block. The energy of the day had shifted, no longer the frenetic rush of excitement but a calmer, more settled feeling. He sat on a bench and watched the last groups of students make their way across the pathways, their laughter still echoing in the warm evening air.

Looking around, Arjun felt a sense of pride swell in his chest. This place... this campus... it felt like home already. He couldn't help but smile to himself, the excitement of the day still humming softly beneath the surface.

Arjun (softly, to himself): "Yeah... I'm going to love it here."

CHAPTER II

CLASHING FIRST IMPRESSIONS

The morning sun bathed the campus in a warm glow as Arjun made his way toward D Block for his first official class. The excitement from yesterday still buzzed inside him, but now, it was laced with a bit of nervous anticipation. As he crossed the wide, tree-lined pathways, he couldn't help but notice the elegant yet imposing architecture that surrounded him, red-brick buildings with towering columns and large windows that exuded both history and prestige.

Arjun (thinking):*This place feels like it's been here forever. Like it's seen generations pass through its halls.*

Amity's campus wasn't just vast; it was crafted with precision. The buildings weren't just functional; they were statements. Statements of power, tradition, and academia. The whole atmosphere demanded excellence, and Arjun felt its weight in every step he took.

D Block came into view, its classic design reflecting a blend of old-world charm and modern functionality. Students streamed in and out, filling the air with chatter and laughter. Arjun climbed the marble staircase to the second floor, where his first class awaited. The walls along the stairwell were lined with art and announcements, but not just any posters, they were professional, meticulously designed, featuring high-profile guest lectures, cutting-edge research symposiums, and prestigious internship opportunities.

As Arjun reached the second floor, he passed a group of international students, their conversations in Chinese adding a cosmopolitan edge to the scene.

Arjun (thinking):*This isn't just a college; it's a global stage.*

Reaching his classroom, Arjun took a deep breath. Yesterday had been the warm-up; today, the real game began. As he stepped inside, the room hummed with a quieter, focused energy. Students were seated in clusters; some engaged in conversation, and others were lost in their phones or laptops. He quickly scanned the room and spotted Yash, who waved him over with a smile.

Yash (grinning): "Hey man, over here! Ready for round two?"

Arjun (smiling, feeling a bit of ease): "Let's hope it's as good as yesterday."

Arjun sat down next to Yash, but just as he started to settle in, a loud voice broke through the general murmur of the room.

Bhati (mocking): "Well, well, if it isn't the new guy! Feeling lost again?"

Arjun turned and immediately recognised Bhati, the athletic-looking guy from yesterday, with an arrogant grin. Bhati was the kind of person who seemed to carry his superiority like a trophy. Flanked by his usual entourage, Bhati leaned back in his chair, his eyes locked on Arjun.

Bhati (smirking): "You sure you're in the right place? Maybe you'd be more comfortable down the hall, intro to survival or something."

The group around him snickered, clearly enjoying the show. Arjun's stomach tightened for a moment, but he straightened his posture, refusing to be rattled.

Arjun (calmly, meeting Bhati's gaze): "I think I'll manage just fine."

Bhati (leaning forward slightly): "That so? Well, just make sure you're not in my seat. Or my way."

Arjun held his gaze for a beat longer before turning back to Yash, who raised an eyebrow but said nothing. Bhati chuckled, clearly pleased with himself, and turned back to his group, resuming his loud conversation.

Yash (whispering): "Don't mind him. Bhati's all talk; he thinks he runs this place just because his family has some money and connections. Best to steer clear when you can."

Arjun (nodding): "I figured. Thanks."

As the classroom filled up, the diversity of students became more apparent. Arjun noticed Naomi and Marban sitting near the front, both from the North East, their features distinct, their energy bright and positive. Rumour had it Marban came from an influential family, but unlike Bhati, he carried his status lightly, his demeanour warm and approachable. Across the room, two girls, Ananya and Anushka, were engrossed in conversation, their laughter cutting through the tense atmosphere Bhati had left behind.

Suddenly, the door opened, and the room seemed to collectively hold its breath.

Ishika Kapoor entered the room, moving with the grace and poise of someone accustomed to attention. Her long, dark hair cascaded over her shoulders, perfectly framing her sharp features. She wore a crisp, tailored blazer over a simple top and jeans, a look that was both effortless and sophisticated. The sunlight streaming through the windows seemed to catch her at just the right angle, making her skin glow.

Arjun (thinking):*Who is she?*

Ishika's mere presence seemed to shift the energy of the room. Heads turned, and conversations paused. She moved through the space as if it belonged to her, barely acknowledging anyone around her as she took a seat near the front.

Yash (leaning in, whispering): "That's Ishika Kapoor. You'll hear a lot about her. She is at the top of the social food chain, gorgeous, and apparently untouchable."

Arjun nodded, intrigued but cautious. Ishika's confidence was magnetic, but there was something about her cool indifference that left him feeling unsettled.

Arjun (thinking):*She's beautiful, sure. But there's something about her... something that feels a bit too distant, too unapproachable.*

As the students settled back into their seats, the professor walked in, his entrance cutting through the last whispers of conversation. The room shifted from social to academic in an instant. The professor, an older man with sharp eyes and a voice that commanded attention began the lecture, diving into the material with ease.

Despite the earlier tension with Bhati, Arjun found himself engrossed in the lecture. The content was challenging but fascinating, and the professor's passion for the subject was contagious. Arjun scribbled notes diligently, his focus locked on every word. The world outside the classroom faded into the background.

By the time the class ended, Arjun felt energised, and his earlier nerves dissipated. As he gathered his things, Yash turned to him with a smile.

Yash: "Not bad for first class, right?"

Arjun (grinning): "Better than I expected."

As they made their way toward the door, Bhati walked past, throwing a glance in Arjun's direction, but this time, there was no comment. It was a small victory, but it felt significant.

Once outside, Yash clapped Arjun on the back.

Yash (smiling): "Hey, don't let Bhati get to you. He's just testing the waters. Stick around with the right people, and you'll be fine."

Arjun (nodding, feeling more at ease): "I'll keep that in mind."

As Yash walked off to meet some other students, Arjun lingered for a moment, taking in the campus around him. The imposing buildings, the neatly manicured lawns, the clusters of students, all of it felt like a world of its own. A world where he would have to navigate both academics and social dynamics, each as complex as the other.

Arjun (thinking):*This is just the beginning. The challenges are real, but so are the opportunities. I'm ready for this.*

With a renewed sense of determination, Arjun set off toward his next class, ready to face whatever came his way.

CHAPTER III

A NIGHT OF SECRETS

The night was alive with anticipation as the students of Amity College prepared for the freshers' party at Privi. The exclusive club, tucked inside the luxurious Shangri-La Hotel in Delhi, was known for its glitzy crowd, a playground for celebrities, socialites, and the city's elite. Tonight, however, it belonged to the freshers of Amity, each one eager to make their mark in a place where appearances spoke louder than words.

Scene: Outside Privi Club, Shangri-La Hotel, Delhi

Ananya (excited): "Can you believe we're actually here? Privi Club! This place is legendary."

Sakshi (grinning): "I know, right? The best of the best. They say Bollywood stars party here."

Vidhi (adjusting her dress): "Well, tonight it's our turn. Let's make it a night to remember."

The girls were dressed to impress, with sparkling dresses, flawless makeup, and the kind of confidence that only an evening at Privi could bring. The valet, quick on his feet, hurried to park the stream of high-end cars, pulling up one after another: sleek black Mercedes, polished BMWs, and the occasional exotic supercar, each more striking than the last.

Anushka (looking around): "Where's Arya? He said he'd meet us here."

Sakshi (rolling her eyes): "You know him. Probably making some dramatic entrance, as usual."

Just then, the deep rumble of an engine announced the arrival of Arya. His sleek black Audi A6 glided to a stop at the kerb. Arya stepped out, dressed in a perfectly tailored suit that radiated sophistication. His smile was that of a man who knew he owned the night.

Arya (grinning): "Ladies, your knight in shining armour has arrived."

Vidhi (playfully): "More like a playboy in a shiny car."

Arya (laughing): "Guilty as charged. But hey, we're here to have fun, aren't we?"

Arya's reputation as the campus playboy preceded him. His confidence was matched only by his love for the spotlight. The Audi was part of his persona, a polished exterior meant to impress, to dazzle, and to leave people wondering what lay beneath.

He turned his attention to Ishika, standing slightly apart from the group. She was stunning, as usual, her outfit effortlessly chic, her expression calm and controlled.

Arya (flirting): "Ishika, you look incredible tonight. How about joining me for a drink?"

Ishika (barely glancing at him): "No, thanks."

Her reply was cool, her indifference unmistakable. Arya's grin faltered for a split second before he recovered.

Arya (shrugging): "Your loss. Shall we head in?"

As they walked toward the entrance, another luxury car pulled up, this time a gleaming Mercedes-Benz. The valet rushed to open the door, and the students watched as a sharply dressed young man stepped out, exuding wealth and power.

Naman (whispering to Bhati): "Who's that guy? Looks like he's someone important."

Bhati (scoffing): "Who cares? Probably just another rich kid showing off."

Vicky (chuckling): "Let's see how he plays it inside."

They entered the club, and Privi's interiors were everything they had imagined. The atmosphere was thick with the scent of wealth, dim lighting, plush seating, and soft leather. The bar gleamed with rows of top-shelf liquor, and the dance floor throbbed with energy, packed with bodies moving to the pulse of the music. Crystal chandeliers hung from the ceiling, casting a subtle glow over the entire scene.

Vidhi (looking around in awe): "This place is unreal. We're actually here."

Sakshi (nodding): "Told you. Only the best for Amity's freshers."

They made their way through the club, past a roped-off VIP section. A small commotion had begun near the entrance to the VIP area. Naman, Bhati, and Vicky—rich boys from Amity who were used to getting their way—were facing off with the club owner.

Naman (irritated): "What do you mean we can't go in? We booked this section!"

Club Owner (calmly but firmly): "I'm sorry, gentlemen, but this area is reserved for a special guest tonight."

Bhati (scoffing): "Reserved? For who? Do you know who we are?"

Before the club owner could answer, Arjun appeared, his presence immediately shifting the tension in the room. Dressed in a simple yet perfectly fitted outfit, he carried himself with a quiet confidence that drew attention. He was no stranger to places like Privi, and the club owner greeted him with a respect that wasn't lost on those watching.

Club Owner (warmly): "Mr. Mehta, welcome. Your table is ready. Please, follow me."

Naman, Bhati, and Vicky exchanged shocked looks, their minds racing to comprehend the scene playing out before them.

Vicky (whispering): "How the hell does he know the owner?"

Naman (frowning): "He's pulling some trick. No way he's on the same level as us."

Bhati (glaring): "This isn't over. We'll find out what he's hiding."

From across the room, Ishika observed the scene, her curiosity piqued. Arjun had always seemed different—quieter, more reserved—but tonight, there was something about him that stood out even more. The way the club owner treated him, with deference and respect, made her question everything she thought she knew about him.

Ishika (thinking): *Who are you, Arjun Mehta?*

Meanwhile, Arya, completely oblivious to the tension around him, made his way to the bar with a grin, ordering drinks for his friends.

Arya (to the bartender): "Whisky on the rocks, and keep them coming."

The bartender, familiar with Arya's type, smirked as he poured the drinks.

Bartender (teasing): "Still chasing the impossible, huh? Maybe aim lower this time."

Arya (laughing): "Where's the fun in that?"

Back in the VIP section, Arjun sat quietly, his drink in hand. Despite the lively atmosphere around him, he remained composed, aware of the eyes on him but choosing to stay in the background. This wasn't a new experience for him; he had spent years learning to navigate these kinds of spaces with ease, blending into the luxury while keeping his true self hidden.

Vidhi (curious): "Ishika, do you know that guy? The one who got the VIP treatment?"

Ishika (glancing at Arjun): "Not really. But there's something about him... I can't quite figure it out."

Ananya (intrigued): "He's different. Not like the others."

Sakshi (nodding): "There's definitely a mystery there. I just can't put my finger on it."

As the night wore on, the club became a blur of lights, music, and laughter. The dance floor was packed, the bar buzzed with drink orders, and the energy was electric. But despite the whirlwind of activity, Arjun remained a quiet observer, a steady presence amidst the chaos.

By the time the party began to wind down and the students started filtering out, the questions surrounding Arjun lingered in the air. Who was he, really? And what secrets lay behind his calm, unassuming exterior?

As Ishika stepped into the cool night air, she couldn't shake the feeling that something important had just unfolded, something that would shape her time at Amity in ways she couldn't yet predict.

Ishika (whispering to herself): "There's more to you than meets the eye, Arjun Mehta. And I'm going to find out what it is."

CHAPTER IV

MENTOR'S WISDOM

The sun shone brightly over the sprawling red-brick campus of Amity College. Another day of classes had begun, but for Arjun, the morning had brought its share of challenges. As he walked through the halls of D Block, the subtle sting of snickers and whispers followed him, a lingering effect of the ever-watchful eyes of Bhati and his crowd.

Scene: Outside the Classroom, D Block

Bhati leaned casually against the wall, his eyes glinting with mischief. A few of his friends flanked him, their grins just as mocking.

Bhati (smirking): "Look who it is, the mystery man. How's it going, Arjun? Still trying to figure out how to fit in?"

Arya (laughing): "Or maybe just trying to find a corner to disappear into."

The comments stung, but Arjun kept his gaze forward, refusing to engage. He had learned by now that reacting would only fuel their taunts. A couple of girls nearby giggled at the exchange, their whispers barely contained.

Girl 1 (whispering): "Why does he even bother? He's so out of place."

Girl 2 (laughing): "Yeah, it's almost sad."

Arjun clenched his fists, his resolve threatening to crack. But before the tension could escalate further, a strong voice cut through the chatter like a blade.

Raina Madam (sternly): "That's enough, all of you."

The hallway fell silent immediately as Raina Midha approached, her commanding presence unmistakable. She was known for her sharp mind and even sharper tongue, and she was a professor not to be trifled with. Her gaze was hard as it swept over Bhati and Arya.

Raina Madam (coldly): "Is this how you choose to spend your time? Harassing your fellow students?"

Bhati (quickly, feigning innocence): "No, ma'am. We were just joking around."

Raina Madam (her voice unwavering): "Jokes at someone else's expense have no place here. I suggest you focus on your studies instead."

Her words left Bhati and Arya momentarily stunned, and after an awkward pause, they mumbled apologies and dispersed, leaving Arjun standing there in silence. He felt a mixture of relief and embarrassment as the stares shifted away from him.

Raina Madam (turning to Arjun, her tone softening): "Arjun, isn't it? Walk with me."

Arjun nodded and followed her down the hallway, away from the gossip and judgement of his peers. They entered an empty classroom, where she gestured for him to sit. The room felt strangely sacred in its silence as if stepping into a place where deeper truths could be uncovered.

Scene: Inside the Classroom

Raina Madam sat across from Arjun, her expression thoughtful. For a moment, she simply observed him, and Arjun could feel the weight of her attention as she saw through the layers of uncertainty he had tried to build around himself.

Raina Madam (gently): "I've noticed you in my classes, Arjun. You're quiet, but your understanding runs deep. So why do you let them get to you?"

Arjun sighed, feeling the vulnerability of the moment but allowing himself to open up to her.

Arjun (softly): "It's hard not to, ma'am. They make me feel like I don't belong here."

She nodded as if she had expected this.

Raina Madam (calmly): "Belonging isn't about fitting into their mould. It's about knowing your worth and standing firm in who you are. You have potential, Arjun, don't let them convince you otherwise."

Her words struck a chord deep within him. For the first time in a long while, he felt seen, truly seen, beyond the surface judgements of others. It was as if she had reached into his core and pulled out something sacred, something that had been buried beneath the insecurities and doubts.

Arjun (gratefully): "Thank you, ma'am. I won't forget this."

Raina Madam (smiling): "Good. Now, let's get to class. You've got a lot of work ahead of you."

As they left the classroom, Arjun felt a sense of renewal, as though the weight on his shoulders had lightened. Raina Madam's belief in him gave him the strength to continue, and for the first time, he felt like he might just be able to find his place at Amity.

Scene: The Courtyard

Later, Arjun sat alone on a bench in the courtyard, reflecting on his conversation with Raina Madam. The sun filtered through the branches of the trees above, casting dappled shadows on the ground. Despite the earlier confrontation, there was peace in the air, a sense of sacredness in the quiet moments between the rush of campus life.

Anushka and Yash approached him, their expressions concerned but warm.

Anushka (gently): "Hey, Arjun. We heard about what happened earlier. Are you okay?"

Arjun forced a smile, grateful for their presence.

Arjun (with a hint of humour): "Just another day in paradise."

Yash sat down beside him, a comforting hand on his shoulder.

Yash (reassuring): "Don't let those idiots get to you. They're not worth your time."

Anushka (nodding): "Exactly. You've got people who care about you, Arjun. Focus on that."

Looking at his friends, Arjun felt a swell of gratitude. He had been feeling so isolated, but their support reminded him that he wasn't as alone as he had thought.

Arjun (sincerely): "Thanks, guys. I appreciate it."

Anushka grinned, her usual cheerfulness shining through.

Anushka (excited): "Speaking of good news, have you heard about the Sangathan competition?"

Yash's eyes lit up at the mention of it.

Yash (enthusiastically): "It's like the Olympics for Amity. Every branch participates, even the international ones. It's massive!"

Arjun's curiosity was piqued.

Arjun (intrigued): "Sangathan? What's that all about?"

Before they could explain further, Ankita Madam appeared in the courtyard, her voice carrying authority as she addressed the gathering of students.

Ankita Madam (announcing): "Attention, everyone! Sangathan is upon us. This is our annual sports competition where all branches of Amity, both national and international, come together to compete. It's a celebration of sportsmanship, unity, and excellence."

A murmur of excitement spread through the courtyard as students began whispering among themselves.

Ankita Madam (continuing): "This year, we're selecting captains to lead our teams. Anushka and Arjun, you've been chosen as sports captains for our branch. Congratulations!"

Arjun was stunned. He glanced at Anushka, who was already beaming.

Anushka (excitedly): "Looks like we'll be working together, Arjun! This is going to be amazing."

Yash clapped Arjun on the back, and his pride is evident.

Yash (grinning): "Congrats, man! You're going to kill it."

Though a sense of pride filled him, Arjun couldn't help but feel a pang of anxiety. Being chosen as a captain was an honour, but it also came with pressure. However, as he looked at his friends, the support in their eyes strengthened his resolve.

Arjun (determined): "Thanks, everyone. Let's make this Sangathan unforgettable."

As the courtyard began to clear, Arjun caught sight of Ishika standing with Bhati's group. She was laughing at something Bhati had said, but her gaze wandered across the courtyard, briefly locking with Arjun's. Her expression was unreadable—indifferent, almost detached—but the moment lingered with him.

Anushka (noticing his distraction): "Don't worry about them. We've got bigger things to focus on."

Arjun nodded, letting thoughts of Bhati and Ishika fade into the background. He had a new challenge ahead, one that would test his resolve and leadership. With Raina Madam's mentorship, the unwavering support of his friends, and the honour of leading in Sangathan, Arjun knew he was on the path to proving something important to himself.

As the sun dipped below the horizon, casting long shadows across the campus, Arjun felt a deep sense of purpose. Maybe, just maybe, he was finally finding his place at Amity.

CHAPTER V

SPIRIT OF SANGATHAN

The buzz around campus was electric. Sangathan, the most anticipated event of the year, was in full swing. Every corner of Amity College brimmed with excitement; banners fluttered in the breeze, students donned their team colours, and the air hummed with the sounds of whistles, cheers, and rallying cries. For many, this wasn't just a competition; it was an opportunity to showcase their grit, athleticism, and, above all, the pride they had in their college.

Sangathan was like no other event at Amity; it was a grand spectacle, almost sacred in its tradition, and a celebration of sportsmanship that involved every branch of the college, including international campuses. The competition was monumental, and the stakes were high. For the students, it wasn't just about winning; it was about earning respect, both on and off the field.

Scene: On the Volleyball Court

Arjun stood at the edge of the volleyball court, his nerves tightly wound. The afternoon sun beat down, casting long shadows over the sand. Around him, the stands were packed with students, their energy palpable as they cheered on their teams. Sangathan was in full throttle, and the excitement was infectious.

His team was warming up, their movements fluid but tense. Arjun had led them through intense training sessions, building not just their skill but their trust in one another. Now, it was time to see if it would pay off.

Anushka (walking up, smiling): "How are you feeling? Ready to crush it?"

Arjun glanced at her, managing a smile of his own despite the tightness in his chest.

Arjun: "We'll give it everything we've got. The team's worked hard; I just hope it's enough."

Anushka (patting him on the shoulder): "It will be. You've been a great captain, Arjun. Just keep them focused."

The crowd roared as the match began, the electric atmosphere charged with anticipation. The stadium lights gleamed down on the court, illuminating every bead of sweat, every tense muscle, every look of determination. **Arjun's** team, clad in red and black, stood together with a fierce resolve. Their opponents were taller and more experienced, but **Arjun's** team had something special, heart.

The whistle blew, and the game burst into motion. **Keshav** served first, his powerful strike sending the ball zipping over the net. The opposing team was quick, but **Vishal** leapt, arms stretched out, blocking the return with a solid smack.

Keshav (shouting as the ball soared back into play): "That's it! Keep pushing!"

Arjun, in the thick of it, directed the flow like a maestro conducting an orchestra. He passed to **Vicky**, who slammed a spike across the court, sending their side of the stadium into uproarious cheers.

Arjun (with urgency): "Eyes on the ball! Stay sharp!"

The first set was theirs in no time, 25-18. Every move they made seemed effortless, their coordination seamless, as though they were communicating through instinct alone. The energy was palpable, and the crowd fed off it.

But in the second set, the tides began to shift. The opposing team, stunned by the early dominance, dug in their heels. Their middle blocker, towering over the net, sent powerful spikes that were nearly impossible to defend. **Vishal** dived for the ball, barely managing to save it with the tip of his fingers.

Vishal (panting after scrambling to keep the ball in play): "They're pressing hard, man!"

Keshav, back on serve, wiped sweat from his brow. He looked at **Arjun**, his eyes serious.

Keshav: "They're closing the gap. We need to adjust."

Arjun nodded, his mind racing and searching for a strategy.

Arjun (breathing hard but steady): "Switch to quick sets, keep them guessing. We can't let them settle into a rhythm."

The rally intensified. The opposition began clawing their way back, point by point. Their hits became harder, their blocks firmer. The sound of shoes squeaking against the polished floor mixed with the rhythmic thud of the ball being struck. Every point felt like a battle.

A timeout was called with the score at 22-23, their lead slipping away. **Arjun's** team huddled together, breathless, hearts pounding.

Keshav (exhausted but determined): "We've still got this. We just need to keep our heads clear."

Vicky (frustrated): "They're reading us too well now. We need to throw something different at them."

Arjun looked at his teammates, all of them exhausted but full of fight. His voice was calm and authoritative, cutting through the chaos.

Arjun: "Stick to the plan. Let's stay smart. Keep the pressure on them, and don't lose focus."

The whistle blew again, and the players returned to the court. But despite their best efforts, the opposing team took the second set, 23-25. The crowd's roar was now mixed with tension and anticipation. The final set loomed.

The third set was a war of nerves. Both teams fought tooth and nail for every point, diving, blocking, and spiking with all the energy they had left.

At 10-9, **Keshav** hit a serve that seemed perfect, but the opposition's defence held firm, sending the ball back with a powerful spike. **Vicky** leapt to block it, but it grazed his fingertips and shot past him.

Keshav (frustrated, under his breath): "Damn it!"

Arjun, sweating and breathless, wiped his face with his jersey.

Arjun (gritting his teeth): "Let it go, focus on the next one. We're still in this."

The tension in the air was almost tangible. The score climbed to 15-15, then 16-16, each side refusing to yield. The crowd was on the edge of their seats, eyes glued to the court, breaths held with every rally.

Vishal (calling out across the court): "Get ready for the set, **Arjun**!"

Arjun leapt into the air, spiking the ball with all the force he could muster. The ball sped toward the opponent's side, but their libero dived, somehow managing to keep it in play. They returned it swiftly, and despite **Keshav**'s valiant attempt at defence, the ball clipped the edge of his fingers and dropped to the ground.

The opposing team took the match, 17-16.

The sound of the whistle blew, signalling the end, and for a brief moment, the crowd fell into a stunned silence. Then, applause erupted, honouring the incredible effort of both teams. But for **Arjun's** side, the sting of defeat was heavy. They had fought so hard, so close, but in the end, it hadn't been enough.

Arjun sank onto the bench, staring at the court, his mind still replaying the final moments. His chest heaved from the effort, and his hands rested limply on his knees. He barely registered the crowd around him as disappointment settled deep in his chest.

A few minutes later, **Anushka** found him, her soft footsteps barely making a sound as she sat beside him on the bench. She didn't say anything at first, just letting the quiet settle between them.

Anushka (gently): "You guys were amazing out there, **Arjun**. You gave it everything."

Arjun (sighing deeply, staring off into the distance): "Yeah, but it stings. We were so close, I could feel it. We were right there."

Anushka watched him for a moment, understanding the weight of his words.

Anushka: "It's always hard when you're that close. But it's not just about winning or losing. You played with heart. People saw that."

Arjun leaned forward, resting his elbows on his knees, still frustrated.

Arjun: "It's just... it feels like we let everyone down. The team, the crowd... I don't know. I keep thinking I should have done more."

Anushka (putting a hand on his arm): "You didn't let anyone down. Not a single person. Everyone out there saw how hard you fought and how much you led the team. That's what matters."

Arjun looked up at her, her words slowly sinking in. He wasn't sure if they made him feel better just yet, but the warmth in her voice helped.

Arjun (nodding slightly): "I guess you're right. It's just hard to shake off that feeling, you know? The 'what ifs.'"

Anushka smiled faintly, her eyes soft and understanding.

Anushka: "You'll drive yourself crazy thinking like that. Don't worry about the 'what ifs.' You played your heart out, and that's what counts. There's always going to be another game, another chance. And next time, you'll be even stronger."

Arjun looked at her for a moment, her confidence in him lifting a small weight from his chest. He leaned back against the bench, letting out a long breath.

Arjun (smiling faintly): "Thanks, **Anushka**. I needed that."

Anushka (teasingly, as she stood up): "Of course you did. Now come on, captain. We've got other things to celebrate."

Arjun chuckled softly, getting up from the bench. The defeat still lingered, but there was a new sense of calm. They walked off the court together, the buzz of the match slowly fading behind them, but the fire inside **Arjun** was far from extinguished. There would be other games, other battles, and next time, he knew he'd come back even stronger.

Scene: The Shooting Range

The following day, **Arjun** found himself at the shooting range, the echo of yesterday's match still lingering in his mind. But today, it was different.

Today was about precision, calm, and control. Shooting had always been his sanctuary, a place where the chaos of the world quieted down, leaving only him and the target in a delicate balance. Here, it wasn't about the speed or strength of a team; it was about inner stillness, focus, and his ability to zone in on one goal with laser-like accuracy.

The morning air was crisp, and the quiet hum of competitors preparing for their event filled the air. **Arjun** stood at his station, his rifle resting comfortably in his hands. His eyes traced the outline of the target, but he wasn't really seeing it yet. In his mind, he was already preparing for the moment when the world around him would fade, and all that mattered was the narrow circle of his aim.

Just then, **Yash** walked over, clapping him on the back.

Yash (grinning): "No pressure, man. Just go out there and do what you do best."

Arjun turned and gave a small smile, appreciating the ease with which **Yash** always managed to lighten the mood, even in tense situations. He knew his friend was right; this wasn't about anyone else. This was his moment. Shooting had always been where he excelled the most, a place where his natural calm allowed him to thrive.

Arjun (nodding): "Thanks, man. Time to tune everything else out."

As the whistle signalled the start of the competition, **Arjun**'s world narrowed to the target ahead. His heartbeat slowed as his breath synchronised with the rhythm he had mastered through countless hours of practice. His mind emptied, leaving only the methodical sequence of actions: shouldering the rifle, aligning his sights, holding his breath, and squeezing the trigger with the lightest touch.

One shot. Then another. Each one hit its mark, each more precise than the last. His form was impeccable, and as the competition went on, **Arjun**'s confidence only grew. His hands were steady, his mind calm. He was no longer thinking, just doing, reacting instinctively to the target before him.

Around him, murmurs from other competitors and spectators rippled through the air, but to **Arjun**, they were distant, like background noise in a dream. All he heard was the click of the trigger, the sound of the bullet breaking the air, and the thud of it hitting the target.

With every successful shot, he felt the tension in his shoulders easing, the previous day's disappointment slipping further from his mind. By the time the final whistle blew, **Arjun** had given everything he had, and he knew it had been enough. He glanced briefly at the scoreboard as the judges tallied the scores, his name rising steadily to the top.

When the final scores flashed on the board, **Arjun** stood at the pinnacle, **first place**, gold medallist.

Yash (from the stands, shouting): "That's my man! Knew you had it in you!"

Arjun couldn't help but grin, the weight of the victory settling in. But it wasn't just about standing on the podium; it was about proving to himself that he could rise above doubts and noise. Yesterday's match may have ended in heartbreak, but today, he had redeemed himself.

As he held his gold medal, the familiar voice of **Professor Raina** caught his attention. She approached him, her eyes filled with pride.

Professor Raina (smiling warmly): "Well done, Arjun. You've made us all proud."

Her words carried weight. **Professor Raina** wasn't one to offer empty compliments, and hearing her say those words felt like validation for all the effort he had put in over the years.

Arjun (smiling humbly): "Thank you, ma'am. It feels good to bring something back for the team."

The medal gleamed in the sunlight, but more than the gold around his neck, it was the sense of accomplishment swelling within him that mattered. He had silenced the doubts in his own head. This victory wasn't just for him, it was for his team, his friends, and the faith they had in him.

Professor Raina (patting his shoulder): "You've shown everyone what true resilience looks like. Yesterday might not have gone your way, but today... today, you showed that you can bounce back, no matter what."

Arjun nodded, feeling the truth of her words settle inside him. It wasn't just about the wins or the losses; it was about how you rose after a fall, about the quiet determination to keep pushing forward. He looked at the range one last time, the targets distant but now clear, a reflection of how he viewed life itself, full of challenges but also opportunities to rise above them.

Yash ran up to him, clapping him on the back with even more vigour.

Yash (laughing): "Now that's what I call a comeback! Drinks on me tonight!"

Arjun chuckled, shaking his head but appreciating the gesture.

Arjun (grinning): "You know I'll hold you to that, right?"

As they walked off the range together, **Arjun** glanced down at his medal one last time, feeling a sense of pride not just in the victory but in the journey. There would always be more matches, more competitions, more battles to fight, but for now, this victory was enough. It wasn't just a win; it was proof that he could face adversity and come out stronger, more focused, and more determined than before.

Scene: The Basketball Court

The atmosphere in the stadium was electric as **Anushka** and her girls' basketball team took their positions on the court. The air was thick with the energy of the crowd, the buzz of sneakers squeaking against the hardwood floor, and the rhythmic bounce of basketballs echoing in the space. They had been a dominant force throughout the tournament, steamrolling past most teams with precision and strength. But today, standing across from them was their toughest challenge yet.

The opposing team—taller, faster, and just as hungry for the win—stood like an immovable wall. **Anushka** could feel the tension, her heart pounding as the referee blew the whistle to start the game.

As the ball was tossed into the air for the tip-off, the sound of the crowd swelled. **Ananya** jumped high, her fingertips brushing the ball, but the opposition snagged it, and just like that, the game was on.

The opposing team wasted no time, driving hard into their zone and weaving through the defence with sharp, precise passes. Their speed was overwhelming. **Anushka** sprinted back, shouting commands to her teammates.

Anushka (calling out, eyes scanning the court): "Cover the wings! Close the gaps!"

Ananya and **Sakshi** scrambled to block their respective players, but the opposing guard zipped past them, cutting through the defence like a knife. A quick pass to the centre, and the ball was up—**swish**—the first points of the game went to the opposition.

The scoreboard flickered, **2-0**.

Anushka gritted her teeth, eyes narrowing in focus. This was no ordinary team. They were relentless, pushing the pace every chance they got, forcing **Anushka** and her team to dig deep just to keep up.

As they reset, **Ananya** passed the ball to **Sakshi**, who dribbled down the court, trying to break through the defence. The opposing players pressed hard, their defence suffocating. **Sakshi** swung the ball to **Anushka** on the wing, and with a quick fake, **Anushka** drove toward the basket.

The crowd's roar grew louder, but just as **Anushka** was about to take the shot, a hand came crashing down on the ball, sending it flying out of bounds.

Ananya (panting as she hustled back): "They're everywhere. Can't get any space!"

Anushka (breathing heavily, her voice firm): "Stay with it. We need to move the ball faster."

The next few possessions were a grind. The other team's defence was tight, and every pass felt risky. But slowly, **Anushka** and her team began to find their rhythm. **Sakshi** hit a smooth jumper from the baseline. **Ananya** grabbed a rebound and muscled it back up for two points.

The scoreboard reflected the tug-of-war, **10-10**. But as the minutes ticked down in the first half, the pace only seemed to quicken. The opposing team launched a series of fast breaks, catching **Anushka's** defence flat-footed. **Anushka** could only watch as their lead began to slip away.

By halftime, the score stood at **24-18**, the other team pulling ahead by six points.

Anushka stood with her hands on her knees, her breath heavy, the weight of the game pressing down on her. The coach called for a timeout, and the girls gathered in a huddle, sweat dripping from their faces.

Ananya (wiping her brow, eyes blazing with determination): "We can take them. We just need to tighten our defence. They're scoring too easily in transition."

Sakshi (nodding, catching her breath): "We need to stop letting them run the floor. They're killing us on the fast breaks."

Anushka looked at her team, their faces a mix of exhaustion and determination. She knew they had it in them; they just needed to regroup.

Anushka (her voice steady but intense): "Exactly. Let's show them what we're made of. We've worked too hard to let this slip away. Stay focused, communicate, and stop letting them get easy points."

The whistle blew, signalling the end of the timeout. The second half began, and the intensity ramped up even more. **Anushka**'s team came out stronger, closing gaps in defence and moving the ball faster on offence.

Ananya made a brilliant steal, sprinting down the court and finishing with a layup. The crowd erupted, sensing the momentum shift. **Anushka** followed it up with a smooth three-pointer, and for the first time since the start, they were ahead, **30-29**.

But the opposing team was not one to back down. They retaliated quickly, launching an offensive blitz. Their point guard faked a drive, pulling back to hit a long-range shot, then immediately stole the ball on the next possession, setting up another fast break.

With just five minutes left, the score was tied, **35-35**.

Anushka felt the pressure mounting. Every possession was a battle now, every shot contested, every rebound fought over as if the game depended on it, and in many ways, it did. The noise of the crowd was deafening, the sound of the ball bouncing, shoes squeaking, and players shouting blending into a chaotic symphony of basketball madness.

In the final two minutes, the opposing team pulled ahead again. They hit a couple of clutch shots, capitalising on a brief lapse in **Anushka**'s defence. **Sakshi** tried to answer with a jumper, but it bounced off the rim.

The last seconds ticked away as the other team maintained their slim lead, **38-35**. In one final, desperate attempt, **Anushka** drove to the basket, weaving through defenders, but her layup missed by inches. The buzzer sounded, and just like that, the game was over.

Anushka stood in the middle of the court, hands on her hips, breathing heavily as the sting of the loss hit her like a wave. The cheers of the other team's fans echoed around the gym, but all she heard was the pounding of her own heart.

Anushka (frustrated, her voice low): "We gave it our all, but they were just better today."

Sakshi walked up beside her, putting a hand on her shoulder.

Sakshi (supportively): "You led us well, **Anushka**. We couldn't have asked for a better captain. This was a team effort, and you gave everything you had."

Anushka nodded, her lips pulling into a small, appreciative smile, though the weight of the defeat still lingered. The sting of coming so close but falling short was always hard to shake.

But as she stood there, surrounded by her teammates, she knew they had fought with everything they had, and in the end, that was what mattered. The road to victory wasn't always straight, and sometimes, it took setbacks like this to build something even stronger.

Scene: At the Swimming Pool

Ishika was in her element in the swimming pool. The water was her domain, and she glided through it with grace and power. Her long strokes carried her ahead of her competitors, the distance between her and the rest growing with every surge.

From the sidelines, Bhati and Arya watched, impressed.

Bhati (smirking): "She's going to crush this. There's no one here who can beat her."

Arya (grinning): "Yeah, she's a natural."

Ishika's final stretch left the others far behind, and when her hand touched the wall, the victory was hers, gold medal secured.

Ishika (emerging from the pool, breathing hard, a smile on her face): "That felt good."

Vidhi (cheering): "You were incredible, Ishika! No one even came close."

Scene: The Tug-of-War Competition

Naman, the muscular leader of the tug-of-war team, stood with his teammates, their feet planted firmly in the dirt. The opposing team was strong, but Naman's team had strategy and coordination on their side. The rope strained as both teams pulled with all their might, sweat pouring down their faces.

Naman (grinning, muscles bulging as they pulled): "Come on, boys! This is ours!"

With one final heave, they dragged the opposing team over the line, securing the gold medal. The crowd erupted in cheers as Naman and his team celebrated.

Bhati (clapping Naman on the back): "You killed it out there, Naman. Well done."

Scene: The Weightlifting Event

Bhati himself had been training hard for the weightlifting event, and now it was his turn to step into the spotlight. His face was tense with concentration as he positioned himself under the barbell. Every muscle in his body screamed with effort as he pushed himself to the limit.

Arya (encouragingly): "Come on, Bhati! You've got this!"

With a final burst of strength, Bhati completed the lift, earning himself a silver medal. Though it wasn't the gold he had been aiming for, he was proud of his achievement.

Bhati (panting, smiling): "Silver's not bad. Next time, it'll be gold."

Scene: The Closing Ceremony

As the final day of Sangathan came to an end, the entire Amity team gathered on the field for the closing ceremony. Despite the highs and lows, they had performed admirably. Students from every branch stood side by side, medals gleaming around their necks as the results were announced.

Arjun's team finished second overall, a remarkable achievement considering the fierce competition.

Ankita Madam (addressing the team, pride in her voice): "You've all done exceptionally well. Sangathan isn't just about winning medals; it's about showing heart, determination, and sportsmanship. And you've all exemplified that."

Arjun looked around at his teammates, the sense of camaraderie stronger than ever. He had led them through this journey, and despite the setbacks, he felt a deep sense of pride.

Arjun (reflecting, smiling): "We may not have won it all, but we accomplished something great. I'm proud of what we've done together."

As the team gathered to celebrate their achievements, Yash raised his glass in a toast.

Yash (grinning): "To us! To a great Sangathan and to even greater things ahead!"

The team cheered, their spirits high as the night stretched on. Sangathan had ended, but the bonds forged through the competition would carry them forward through every challenge that lay ahead.

CHAPTER VI

WHISPERS IN THE MOUNTAINS

After the intensity of Sangathan, the students of Amity College were eager for a break. The long-anticipated trip to Dharamshala was the perfect opportunity to unwind and reset. Dharamshala, with its picturesque landscapes and spiritual air, was a world away from the bustling life of the college campus. Excitement buzzed through the hallways as students packed their bags and shared eager conversations about the adventure that awaited them.

But for Arjun, the trip felt like another challenge, a gauntlet of simmering tensions with Bhati's gang and the ever-growing curiosity from his classmates. The mountain retreat wasn't just about relaxation. For Arjun, it seemed that with every passing moment, his secrets were becoming harder to keep.

Scene: On the Bus to Dharamshala

The bus was alive with energy as it snaked its way through the hills, laughter and chatter bouncing around the confined space. The scenic route revealed towering mountains and deep valleys covered in a patchwork of green forests and mist. Students had their faces pressed to the windows, admiring the breathtaking views. But inside the bus, another kind of tension stirred.

Bhati lounged back in his seat, his smirk never far from his face, eyes fixated on Arjun.

Bhati (leaning back, voice dripping with sarcasm): "So, Arjun, how does it feel to be on a trip like this? A bit out of your league, isn't it?"

Arya, seated nearby, grinned and added his own jab.

Arya (mocking): "Yeah, Arjun, I hope you didn't have to sell something just to afford this ride."

The laughter that followed from Bhati's gang felt louder than it was. Arjun kept his gaze on the passing landscape, his jaw tight. He refused to let them get under his skin, even as their jabs cut deeper than he would ever admit.

But it was Ishika's calm and cutting voice that made him tense further.

Ishika (turning in her seat, her tone cool): "Maybe you should have stayed back, Arjun. After all, it's clear you don't really fit in here with the rest of us."

Her words felt like a slap, and for a moment, Arjun's heart sank. He could feel the eyes on him, the scrutiny, the judgment. The air in the bus felt heavy, and even the beautiful scenery outside seemed far away.

Yash (leaning over, speaking quietly): "Ignore them, Arjun. They're just trying to get a reaction out of you."

Anushka, ever the optimist, smiled reassuringly.

Anushka: "Don't let them ruin this. It's going to be great once we get there."

Arjun offered a small smile in return, grateful for their support, but the sting of the insults lingered as the bus continued its ascent into the mountains.

Scene: Arrival at the Five-Star Hotel in Dharamshala

Nestled among the foothills of the Himalayas, the five-star hotel where the students would be staying looked like something out of a dream. Surrounded by towering mountains and dense forests, the hotel's grand facade gleamed in the afternoon sun. As the students disembarked from the buses, their eyes widened in awe at the opulence of their surroundings.

The hotel lobby was a masterpiece of modern luxury, with gleaming marble floors, floor-to-ceiling windows showcasing panoramic views of the mountains, and plush furnishings that invited you to sink into their comfort.

Bhati and his crew, however, couldn't resist taking another shot at Arjun.

Bhati (whispering loudly to Arya): "Bet this place is way out of Arjun's budget."

Arya (laughing): "I wouldn't be surprised if he ends up in the janitor's closet."

As the students filed into the hotel lobby, collecting their room keys, Arjun stepped up to the front desk. The receptionist glanced at her computer screen, her brows furrowing slightly as she read his booking details.

Receptionist (politely, but with a hint of disdain): "It seems there's been a mistake. This room might be more appropriate for you."

She handed him a key to one of the more modest rooms. Before Arjun could respond, a flurry of movement caught his attention. The hotel manager, a well-dressed man with an air of urgency, hurried over.

Hotel Manager (apologetically): "Mr. Mehta, please forgive the confusion. Let me personally escort you to your suite."

The receptionist's eyes widened, and Bhati's group, standing nearby, exchanged puzzled looks.

Bhati (whispering to Arya, confused): "What's going on? Why's the manager treating him like some kind of VIP?"

Arya (frowning): "This doesn't make any sense. He's got to be playing us somehow."

Arjun, feeling the weight of the stares, followed the manager to a private elevator. When they reached his suite, the doors opened to reveal a room unlike any the others would see on this trip. The expansive suite offered sweeping views of the mountains, with sleek, modern decor and every possible luxury at his fingertips. Arjun couldn't help but feel both relief and discomfort. The special treatment was only going to fuel more suspicion.

Scene: Dinner at the Hotel Restaurant

Later that evening, the students gathered for dinner in the hotel's upscale restaurant. The atmosphere was lively, filled with the sounds of laughter and clinking glasses. The room was grand, with floor-to-ceiling windows overlooking the twilight mountains. Chandeliers bathed the space in warm, golden light.

Bhati and Arya, seated at a table with their group, saw an opportunity for more ridicule.

Bhati (loudly, grinning): "So, Arjun, how's the food in the bargain section? Or did they finally upgrade your meal plan?"

Arya (mockingly): "Maybe they threw in a free meal with your room."

Before Arjun could respond, the hotel manager appeared again, this time with a waiter in tow. The room quieted as the manager approached Arjun's table.

Hotel Manager (respectfully): "Mr. Mehta, we've prepared a special menu for you. Please allow us to serve you in our private dining area."

The room went silent as everyone watched Arjun being led to a secluded section of the restaurant, where a lavish spread awaited him. Bhati's group stared in disbelief, their earlier amusement now replaced with confusion and suspicion.

Vicky (whispering to Bhati): "What the hell is going on? How does he rate this kind of treatment?"

Bhati (narrowing his eyes): "He's playing some kind of trick. No way this is legit."

Across the room, Yash and Anushka exchanged glances, their concern growing.

Yash (quietly to Anushka): "This is getting weird. What's going on with Arjun?"

Anushka (shaking her head): "I don't know, but it's clear there's more to him than we thought."

Ishika, watching the entire scene from her table, felt her curiosity deepen. There was something about Arjun that didn't add up. He wasn't like the others, and she was determined to figure out why.

Ishika (thinking to herself): "There's more to you than meets the eye, Arjun. I'm going to figure this out."

Scene: Exploring Dharamshala

The next morning, the group set out to explore the scenic beauty of Dharamshala. The cool mountain air was a refreshing change from the bustling city life. The students visited monasteries, trekked to scenic viewpoints, and browsed through colourful local markets. Despite the picturesque surroundings, tension still simmered beneath the surface.

Arya and Bhati, walking side by side, kept their eyes on Arjun.

Arya (determined): "We've got to figure out what's going on with Arjun. This whole thing doesn't sit right."

Bhati (gritting his teeth): "Don't worry. We will. He can't keep this act up forever."

As they meandered through the market, Arjun found himself alone, admiring a collection of hand-carved wooden statues. Ishika approached him, her expression unreadable.

Ishika (casually): "So, Arjun, how are you enjoying the trip so far?"

Arjun glanced at her, wary of her intentions.

Arjun: "It's fine. The place is beautiful."

Ishika (smirking): "I bet it is. Must feel like quite the upgrade for you, doesn't it?"

Arjun chose not to engage, keeping his tone calm.

Arjun: "I'm just here to enjoy the experience, like everyone else."

For a moment, Ishika studied him, her sharp gaze searching for answers.

Ishika (softly): "You're not like everyone else, though, are you?"

Before Arjun could respond, the rest of the group rejoined them, and the moment passed. But Ishika's words lingered in the air, the unspoken question left hanging.

Scene: Back at the Hotel

That evening, as the students returned to the hotel, the mystery surrounding Arjun was the only topic on Bhati and Arya's minds.

Bhati (frustrated): "There's something he's not telling us. And I'm going to find out what it is."

Arya (nodding): "Yeah, there's no way he's just some regular guy. He's hiding something."

Across the room, Ishika sat quietly, deep in thought.

Ishika (to herself): "Or maybe we're the ones who don't really know him."

The trip that had started as a chance to relax had turned into something far more complicated, a web of intrigue, suspicion, and curiosity. As Arjun lay in his luxurious suite that night, staring up at the ceiling, he couldn't shake the feeling that his carefully constructed facade was beginning to crack. His secrets were becoming harder to keep, and he knew it was only a matter of time before the truth came out.

When it did, everything would change.

CHAPTER VII

SHADOWS OF AFFLUENCE

The room was still buzzing with chatter from the Dharamshala trip as **Sachin Sir** entered, a thoughtful expression on his face. He tapped the table, and the class slowly quieted down.

Sachin Sir: "I hope everyone enjoyed the trip, but today, let's talk about something that struck me during our time there. The mountains, the beauty... and how we're slowly destroying it."

He paused for effect, letting the weight of his words sink in.

Vidhi, always the first to jump in, raised her hand eagerly.

Vidhi: "Sir, Dharamshala is beautiful, but there was garbage everywhere. Plastic bottles, wrappers, even near the rivers! It felt like we were walking through a trash dump, not the mountains."

A few heads nodded in agreement. **Yash**, sitting next to her, added his own observation.

Yash: "It's strange, right? We go to these places to escape city pollution, but people bring their bad habits with them. I saw plastic bags on the hiking trail, too. It's ruining everything."

Ishika, normally quiet in class, chimed in, her voice sharp.

Ishika: "And the worst part is, it's preventable. People treat these places like they can just throw things wherever they want. They don't care about the damage they're doing."

Sachin Sir was pleased with how engaged they were. He leaned forward, his eyes narrowing.

Sachin Sir: "So, what can we do about it? What's the solution?"

There was a brief pause before **Arjun** raised his hand.

Arjun: "Sir, I think it's about education. If people knew the long-term impact, maybe they'd be more careful. But I also think the authorities need to step up. There should be fines for littering."

Sachin, Sir, nodding approvingly: "Good point, Arjun. But enforcement alone isn't enough."

Suddenly, **Arya**, who had been scribbling in his notebook, raised his hand with a grin.

Arya: "Sir, what if we just create a giant vacuum? Like, a huge machine that sucks up all the trash from the mountains!"

For a second, there was silence. Then, the class erupted into laughter.

Vidhi, between fits of laughter: "Arya, we're talking about mountains, not outer space!"

Yash, wiping a tear from his eye: "Yeah because a giant vacuum cleaner will totally fit on the narrow mountain paths."

Even **Sachin Sir** couldn't help but smile, though he quickly brought the discussion back on track.

Sachin, Sir, still smiling: "Alright, alright, let's reel it back in. Although not as... ambitious as Arya's idea, what we can do is raise awareness and be responsible travellers. Small actions like carrying reusable bottles or disposing of trash properly can make a big difference."

The mood shifted back to seriousness as the students absorbed the message. They discussed ideas like promoting eco-tourism, stricter waste disposal regulations, and even organising clean-up drives during future trips.

As the conversation wound down, **Sachin Sir** stood back and watched his students. Despite Arya's joke, there was a genuine concern among them. They were part of a generation that wanted change, that saw the beauty of the mountains but also understood the fragility of nature.

The laughter from earlier was gone, replaced by a quiet resolve.

Sachin Sir: "It's clear that you all care deeply about this. Let's hope that the next time we visit a place like Dharamshala, we'll see cleaner trails and fresher air. Because of that change? It starts with all of us."

The class fell silent, the weight of his words settling over them. It was one thing to talk about change, but to act on it? That was another challenge entirely.

Scene: Zoom Call Between Arjun, Yash, and Anushka

Arjun was looking forward to some quiet time at home when he received a Zoom call from Yash and Anushka. They both appeared on the screen, smiling and clearly excited about something.

Yash: (Grinning) "Hey, Arjun! What's the plan for the break?"

Anushka: (Excitedly) "Yeah, we should totally catch up! Maybe we can visit you in Delhi?"

Arjun felt a pang of hesitation. He had always kept his life in Delhi separate from his college life, and the thought of his friends discovering his secret made him uncomfortable.

Arjun: (Trying to sound casual) "I don't know, guys. Maybe we should just rest and meet up after the break?"

Yash: (Persisting) "Come on, man! We've been through so much together. It'll be fun to hang out without all the college pressure."

Anushka: (Pouting playfully) "Please, Arjun? We won't take no for an answer."

Faced with their enthusiasm, Arjun found it impossible to say no. He sighed, giving in.

Arjun: (Reluctantly) "Alright, alright. Come over. But don't say I didn't warn you; it's not going to be as exciting as you think."

Yash: (Cheering) "That's the spirit! We'll see you soon, buddy."

Scene: Arjun's Home in Golf Links, Delhi

A few days later, Yash and Anushka arrived at Golf Links, one of the most prestigious addresses in Delhi and all of Asia. As their car pulled up to the vast, gated property, they were struck by the sheer opulence of the surroundings. The expansive lawns, meticulously maintained gardens, and luxury cars parked in the driveway made them feel as though they had stepped into a different world.

Anushka: (Gasping) "This... this is your house?"

Yash: (Stunned) "Arjun, you never mentioned you lived in a palace!"

Arjun, who had come out to greet them, looked a bit sheepish. He knew there was no hiding the truth now.

Arjun: (Smiling awkwardly) "Yeah, I guess it is a bit much."

They walked through the grand entrance, the massive wooden doors opening to reveal a foyer decorated with exquisite furniture and art. Everything was premium, including the marble floors, the crystal chandeliers, and the rich textures of the walls.

Yash: (Still in awe) "This place is incredible. How have you managed to keep this a secret?"

Arjun: (Shrugging) "I didn't think it was relevant. It's just... home."

As they wandered through the house, they noticed a large, striking painting hanging on one of the walls. It depicted a scene of nature, with bold colours and intricate details.

Anushka: (Admiring the painting) "This is beautiful. Where did you get it?"

Before Arjun could answer, his father, Karan Mehta, walked into the room. Tall and imposing, with a presence that commanded respect, Karan was clearly someone who had seen and done much in his life.

Karan Mehta: (Smiling) "That painting was a gift from the Minister of Cultural Affairs last year. It's worth millions."

Yash and Anushka exchanged stunned glances. They had known Arjun was different, but they had never imagined the scale of his wealth.

Yash: (Hesitantly) "Arjun, what's going on? This... this is a lot to take in."

Arjun knew it was time to come clean. He led them to a quiet sitting area where they could talk in private.

Arjun: (Taking a deep breath) "There's something I haven't told you guys. My family... we're not exactly normal."

Anushka and Yash listened intently as Arjun explained his family's background. He told them about his father's connections, his involvement with a powerful political organisation when it was led by a prominent leader, and how that friendship had helped his father build a massive, albeit somewhat shady, business empire.

Arjun: (Continuing) "My dad is known as the Hawala King of India. His business deals in large sums of money, moving it around the world in ways that aren't exactly legal. It's not something I'm proud of, but it's the reality I grew up with."

Anushka and Yash were silent for a moment, processing what they had just heard.

Anushka: (Gently) "Why didn't you tell us earlier, Arjun? We're your friends."

Yash: (Nodding) "Yeah, we wouldn't have judged you. We just want to understand."

Arjun looked at them, grateful for their understanding.

Arjun: (Sincerely) "I didn't want you to see me differently. I wanted to be just Arjun, not the son of some rich guy with a questionable business. But now that you know, I need you to promise me something."

They leaned in, listening closely.

Arjun: (Serious) "Please don't tell anyone about this. I don't want this getting out. It's already hard enough keeping it under wraps at college."

Yash and Anushka looked at each other, then back at Arjun. They could see how much this meant to him.

Anushka: (Softly) "We promise, Arjun. Your secret is safe with us."

Yash: (Firmly) "Absolutely. We've got your back."

Arjun felt a wave of relief wash over him. His friends had seen the truth, and they had accepted him for who he was. It was more than he could have hoped for.

Karan Mehta: (Entering the room with a smile) "Good to see you kids getting along so well. Make yourselves at home. We're all family here."

As the evening wore on, the initial shock began to fade, replaced by the warmth of friendship. Arjun knew that, no matter what happened, he could count on Yash and Anushka to stand by him. And that, more than anything, made him feel truly at home.

Interlude: Anticipations

The first year at Amity College had passed in a whirlwind, leaving behind a trail of memories that would be etched into the minds of its students forever. Friendships had been forged in the corridors of D Block, rivalries had sparked on the sports fields, and secrets had been whispered in quiet corners of the campus. Arjun, who had once walked these grounds as a nervous freshman, now stood at the cusp of his second year, no longer a stranger to the complexities of college life.

The journey so far had been anything but ordinary. From the highs of Sangathan, where victories were celebrated and losses were mourned, to the quiet moments of introspection, each experience had shaped the person he was becoming. The bonds he had formed with Yash and Anushka had grown stronger, but the undercurrents of tension and unspoken truths lingered, threatening to reshape those very connections.

As the second year loomed, a sense of anticipation hung in the air. The students of Amity knew that the days ahead would bring new challenges academically, socially, and personally. Friendships would be tested, alliances would shift, and the once-clear lines between friend and foe would blur. The campus, with its sprawling lawns and imposing red-bricked buildings, would become a stage for the unfolding drama of their lives.

How would they cope with the pressures of what was to come? Would they stand by each other, or would the weight of their secrets and ambitions drive them apart? The answers lay in the days ahead, in the choices they would make, and in the paths they would choose to follow.

As the students prepared to step into their second year, one thing was certain: nothing would remain the same. The story that had begun with tentative steps was now set to dive into deeper waters, where the true nature of their characters would be revealed, and where the consequences of their actions would be impossible to ignore.

The first year is over, but the book is far from finished. And with each turn of the page, the stakes would only grow higher.

CHAPTER VIII

FAULT LINES

The sky was a dull, brooding grey, with thick clouds stretching endlessly overhead. There wasn't a single sliver of sunlight breaking through the heavy curtain. **Arjun** stood by the window, staring out at the overcast sky. The usual warmth of the sun was nowhere to be found, and the day felt as though it was draped in shadows over Amity College as the new academic session began. The first year had come to an end, and with it, a new wave of energy and challenges swept through the campus. Arjun, however, couldn't shake off the feeling of unease that lingered as he walked through H Block, where students were gathering to catch up after the break.

Scene: H Block, Amity College

The courtyard buzzed with conversations and laughter, but Arjun felt a familiar tension in the air. It wasn't long before Bhati and Naman noticed him.

Bhati: (Leaning against a wall, smirking) "Well, if it isn't our silent friend. Still too shy to speak up, Arjun?"

Naman: (Chuckling) "Or maybe he's just waiting for someone to save him. Again."

Arjun's friends, Yash and Anushka, were nearby and caught wind of the remarks. Yash, with his usual calm demeanour, placed a reassuring hand on Arjun's shoulder.

Yash: (Gently) "Don't let them get to you, Arjun. They're just trying to get under your skin."

Anushka: (Frowning) "You should really stand up to them. You don't have to take this. You're stronger than they think."

Arjun gave them a small, appreciative smile. He admired Yash's calmness and Anushka's spirited nature, but he knew confronting Bhati and Naman would only escalate things.

Arjun: (Softly) "It's okay. I'm here for my studies, not to start fights."

Anushka, always full of energy, wasn't convinced but respected his decision.

Anushka: (Sighing) "You're too nice, Arjun. But we're here for you, just so you know."

Yash nodded in agreement, his calm presence offering a quiet strength that Arjun often found comforting.

Scene: Pan Shop Outside Campus

Later that day, Arjun decided to step out for a break and headed to a nearby pan shop just outside the campus. The small shop was a popular hangout spot for students, and as Arjun approached, he noticed Arya and Vicky leaning against the counter, smoking.

Arya: (Smirking) "Look who's here, the quiet little mouse. What's the matter, Arjun? Need a cold drink to cool off from all the studying?"

Vicky: (Nervously laughing) "Yeah, maybe a cold drink will help him grow some courage."

Arjun, tired of the constant teasing, decided not to stay silent this time.

Arjun: (Firmly) "Why don't you just leave me alone? I'm not bothering you."

Arya and Vicky exchanged glances, surprised by his response.

Arya: (Mockingly) "Oh, so you've found your voice, huh? Let's see how long it lasts."

Vicky: (Worriedly) "Guys, maybe we should just leave it. I don't want any trouble."

Arya: (Scoffing) "Come on, Vicky, don't be such a chicken. It's just Arjun."

The argument quickly escalated, voices rising as tensions flared. Arya, feeling challenged, pulled out his phone and made a call.

Arya: (On the phone, with a sneer) "Bhati, get over here. We've got a situation."

Within minutes, Bhati arrived in his car with Naman by his side. The two of them stepped out, their expressions darkening as they saw Arjun standing alone.

Bhati: (Menacingly) "What's going on here? Arjun causing trouble?"

Naman: (Grinning) "Looks like he needs another lesson."

Before Arjun could react, Bhati and Naman grabbed him, pushing him around while Arya and Vicky looked on. Vicky, clearly uncomfortable, tried to speak up.

Vicky: (Hesitantly) "Guys, maybe we should just let it go. My family's strict, and I don't want to get into any mess."

Arya: (Laughing) "Relax, Vicky. It's just a little fun."

As the situation escalated, a police officer who had been patrolling the area noticed the commotion and rushed over.

Police Officer: (Sternly) "What's going on here? Break it up, all of you!"

Seeing the officer, Bhati and his group reluctantly let go of Arjun, but their expressions remained defiant.

Bhati: (Smirking) "Nothing, sir. Just teaching this guy a lesson."

Naman: (Sarcastically) "Yeah, just a friendly chat."

Police Officer: (Firmly) "All of you, come with me. We're going to the station."

Bhati: (Mockingly) "Oh, we're going to the station now? Looks like you're in for it, Arjun."

Scene: Police Station

At the police station, the atmosphere was tense as the group was brought in. The constable who had brought them in was a good friend of Bhati's father, and it showed in the way he handled the situation.

Constable: (Glaring at Arjun) "So, you're the one causing trouble, huh? Picking fights with decent people?"

Bhati and the others quickly jumped in, accusing Arjun of starting the fight.

Bhati: (Feigning innocence) "We were just minding our business, sir, and this guy comes along and starts mouthing off."

Arya: (Backing him up) "Yeah, we were just having a chat, and he started acting up."

Vicky: (Nervously) "I... I didn't really see how it started, sir."

The constable, clearly biased, was about to strike Arjun with his stick when the Station House Officer (SHO) arrived.

SHO: (Impatiently) "What's going on here?"

The constable, eager to impress, explained the situation, placing all the blame on Arjun. The SHO, who knew Bhati's family well, turned to Arjun with a scowl.

SHO: (Scolding) "You think you can just come here and start fights? You're lucky I don't throw you in a cell right now."

As the constable raised his stick to strike Arjun, Arjun spoke up, his voice calm but firm.

Arjun: (Quietly) "Please, call Mr. Srivastav."

The SHO paused, looking at Arjun with suspicion.

SHO: (Curiously) "How do you know Commissioner Srivastav?"

Arjun: (Calmly) "Just call him. He'll clear things up."

The SHO hesitated, not believing Arjun's claim. He nodded to the constable to proceed, but just then, the phone on the SHO's desk rang. The SHO answered, and his expression changed immediately.

SHO: (On the phone) "Yes, sir... Yes, sir... Of course, sir. Right away, sir."

The SHO hung up, his demeanour completely altered. He looked at Arjun with a mix of shock and respect.

SHO: (To the constable) "Release him immediately. And show him some respect."

The constable, confused but obedient, stepped back. The SHO turned to Arjun.

SHO: (Respectfully) "Mr. Srivastav has instructed us to release you with respect. You're free to go."

Everyone in the room was stunned, especially Bhati and his friends. The SHO then turned to Bhati and the others.

SHO: (Firmly) "The rest of you stay here."

Arjun, who had been silent throughout, finally spoke up.

Arjun: (Politely) "Please release them as well. It was just a misunderstanding."

The SHO hesitated but then nodded, allowing the others to go as well. As they left the station, Vicky walked alongside Arjun, his expression thoughtful.

Vicky: (Softly) "Thanks, Arjun. I didn't expect that. My family would've killed me if I got into serious trouble."

Arjun: (Nodding) "No problem, Vicky. Just be careful next time."

As they stepped outside, Arjun turned to the constable who had recognised him and called the commissioner.

Arjun: (Sincerely) "Thank you for your help, officer. I appreciate it."

The constable nodded, still slightly taken aback by the whole situation.

As they walked away from the station, the dynamics had clearly shifted. Vicky's attitude had softened towards Arjun, but Bhati and Naman's hatred for him had only deepened. The heavy clouds above mirrored the tense atmosphere as **Arjun** and the others finally walked out of the police station. The cool wind brushed past them, but no one spoke.

The events inside had left everyone shaken, especially with the sudden intervention from **Arjun's** connection to the police commissioner. But as they stepped into the dull, overcast morning, **Bhati** walked with a smirk, his posture still arrogant despite what had transpired.

Bhati's family had always had deep roots in politics. His father, a local MLA, wielded immense influence over the city's administration, and his family name was enough to open doors that most could never even knock on. The police knew who **Bhati** was, and most of them preferred to stay out of his way. In many ways, it had shaped him into the entitled, ruthless person he is today.

Born into privilege, **Bhati** had never known what it meant to struggle. Growing up, he saw how his father manipulated situations and how politics was more about power than service. It fascinated him. Unlike his classmates, who were planning careers in business or engineering, **Bhati's** path was clear: he was going to follow his father into politics.

It wasn't just a desire to be a politician; **Bhati** wanted power. Real power. He craved the control his father had, and he had no intention of settling for anything less. He often boasted to his friends that, one day, he would rise even higher than his father, aiming for positions of national influence. Joining politics, for **Bhati**, was a way to ensure that his name would be feared and respected.

But beneath all that arrogance lay a deep-seated insecurity. **Bhati** knew that his family's reputation gave him a head start, but he also feared that if he didn't prove himself, he would forever be stuck in his father's shadow. That was why he wanted to show strength, even in situations like today's incident at the police station. He couldn't afford to look weak, not to his friends, not to anyone.

As they walked toward their cars, **Bhati**, still fuming from how things had turned out and, made a vow to himself. One day, people like **Arjun** wouldn't have the luxury of pulling strings. He would make sure of it.

CHAPTER IX

DEBATE

It was a typical bustling morning on campus. The sun, hidden behind a few scattered clouds, cast a warm glow over the pathways as students hurried between classes. The soft hum of chatter filled the air, with groups of friends lounging under the shade of trees or making their way to the crowded D Block café. Volleyball practice was in full swing on the courts, and a few others were jogging around the field, their laughter occasionally breaking through the background noise.

Near the notice board, a small group of students was gathered, chatting and exchanging notes, when **Marban** walked by. His attention was immediately drawn to the bright red poster that had just been pinned up.

Marban, stopping abruptly and reading out loud: "Debate competition... 'Capitalism–For or Against'."

A grin spread across his face as he turned around, catching sight of **Yash** and **Vidhi** walking toward him.

Marban, raising his voice: "Guys! Check this out!"

Yash, raising an eyebrow, looked curious as he approached. **Vidhi** squinted at the notice, leaning in closer.

Vidhi, with a slight smirk: "Debate competition, huh? I knew they'd throw something like this at us eventually."

More students gathered as **Marban**'s excitement spread through the group. **Ishika** and **Ananya**, overhearing the chatter, made their way over as well. The notice board quickly became the centre of attention, and within minutes, everyone was talking about the upcoming event.

Yash, reading the topic again: "Capitalism—For or Against. Looks like we've got some thinking to do."

The campus, once filled with idle conversations and laid-back energy, suddenly felt alive with anticipation for the debate.

The announcement of a debate competition spread through the class like wildfire. The topic was capitalism, a subject that promised to ignite fierce opinions and intense discussions. Ankita Madam, known for her strict yet fair approach, stood at the front of the classroom, her gaze sweeping over the eager faces of her students.

Ankita Madam: (Firmly) "The topic for our debate is capitalism. I expect well-researched arguments. Who is for the motion?"

A few hands shot up immediately. Vidhi, always confident and outspoken, was the first to speak.

Vidhi: (With conviction) "I'm for the motion. Capitalism drives progress and innovation."

Beside her, Ishika nodded in agreement, a determined glint in her eyes.

Ishika: (Coolly) "Count me in. It's the backbone of a thriving economy."

Ananya and Bhati also raised their hands, clearly aligned with Vidhi and Ishika.

Ananya: (Smiling) "Absolutely. It's what keeps the world moving forward."

Bhati: (Smirking) "It's about the survival of the fittest. Only the strong deserve to succeed."

Ankita Madam nodded, then looked around the room.

Ankita Madam: (Challengingly) "And who will argue against the motion?"

For a moment, there was silence. Then, slowly, Arjun raised his hand.

Arjun: (Calmly) "I'm against the motion. Capitalism, unchecked, leads to exploitation and inequality."

The class buzzed with surprise. Ishika's eyes narrowed as she looked at Arjun, clearly not expecting him to take such a stand. Ankita Madam turned to the rest of the class.

Ankita Madam: (Encouragingly) "Any more participants?"

Yash, who had been quietly observing, raised his hand with a thoughtful expression.

Yash: (Steadily) "I'll join Arjun. There's more to this than just profit."

Anushka, always supportive and ready for a challenge, nodded firmly.

Anushka: (Determinedly) "Me too. We need to talk about the human cost."

There was a brief pause before Vicky, still a bit nervous from the previous incident, raised his hand.

Vicky: (Quietly) "I'm in. Let's do this."

With the teams set, the atmosphere in the class shifted. Everyone knew this was going to be more than just an academic exercise; it was a battle of ideals.

Scene: The Day of the Debate

The classroom was packed, students filling every seat as they awaited the debate. The tension was palpable as the two teams prepared their final arguments.

Vidhi, Ishika, Ananya, and Bhati took their places, exuding confidence. Arjun, Yash, Anushka, and Vicky stood across from them, their expressions determined and focused.

Ankita Madam signalled the start of the debate, and Vidhi began with her opening statement.

Vidhi: (Passionately) "Capitalism is the engine of innovation. It rewards hard work, drives progress, and allows individuals to rise based on merit. It's the system that has liftcd millions out of poverty and created opportunities for countless others."

The applause was immediate. Vidhi's words resonated with many in the room.

Then it was Arjun's turn. He stood, his voice calm but with an undercurrent of intensity.

Arjun: (Firmly) "Capitalism may drive innovation, but it also creates deep inequalities. It rewards those who already have it while pushing those who do not have it to the margins. It's a system that often values profit over people, leading to exploitation and suffering."

The room fell silent, the weight of his words hanging in the air.

As the debate continued, both sides presented their arguments. Ishika, sharp and articulate, countered Arjun's points with a fierce conviction.

Ishika: (Confidently) "The problems you describe aren't inherent to capitalism; they're the result of poor governance. Capitalism, when regulated, can uplift societies. It's about creating a system where everyone has the chance to succeed."

Arjun didn't back down. His gaze locked with Ishika's as he responded.

Arjun: (Sharply) "Regulation isn't a cure-all. The power still lies in the hands of the few. And what about those who are left behind? Those who don't have the resources to compete? Are we just supposed to accept that as the cost of progress?"

The debate grew more heated as the two clashed, their voices rising above the murmurs of the audience. The intensity between Arjun and Ishika was palpable, each pushing the other to defend their beliefs with more fervour.

Ishika: (Challengingly) "So what's your solution, Arjun? A system where everyone gets a participation trophy? Where mediocrity is rewarded?"

Arjun: (Coldly) "No, Ishika. A system where human dignity isn't sacrificed at the altar of profit.

Where the value of a person isn't measured by their bank account."

The room was electric, the tension so thick it was almost tangible. The other students watched in silence, captivated by the intensity of the exchange.

Finally, Raina Madam, who had been observing quietly from the back, stepped forward.

Raina Madam: (Calmly but firmly) "That's enough. The debate is over. We've heard both sides."

Her voice cut through the tension, bringing the room back to reality. The students sat back, the atmosphere still charged from the confrontation.

Ankita Madam stepped forward to announce the results.

Ankita Madam: (Evenly) "Both sides presented compelling arguments, but after careful consideration, the team against the motion has won this debate."

Arjun's team exchanged glances, their expressions a mix of relief and satisfaction. On the other side, Ishika's face was unreadable, though a hint of frustration flickered in her eyes.

Scene: Later at D Block

After the debate, as the students dispersed, Arjun found himself walking alone through D Block. He hadn't expected to run into Ishika, but there she was, standing near the notice board, seemingly lost in thought.

Their eyes met, and for a moment, there was a silence that spoke volumes. Finally, Ishika spoke.

Ishika: (Softly) "That was... intense. I didn't expect you to argue like that."

Arjun shrugged, his tone neutral.

Arjun: "It was a debate. We both had our points to make."

Ishika nodded, her gaze thoughtful.

Ishika: (Genuinely) "You were good, Arjun. Really good. I guess I underestimated you."

Arjun offered a small, almost imperceptible smile.

Arjun: "You weren't too bad yourself, Ishika."

They stood there for a moment longer, the tension from earlier replaced by a strange sense of mutual respect. As they parted ways, Ishika couldn't help but feel a slight flutter in her chest, an unfamiliar feeling that she couldn't quite place.

For the first time, Arjun was no longer just the quiet boy in the corner. He was something more, something intriguing.

CHAPTER X

WINDS OF CHANGE

As the echoes of the debate competition faded, the students of Amity College settled back into their routines. The campus buzzed with the usual energy, but for Arjun, Yash, and Anushka, things were different. The intensity of the debate had forged a stronger bond between them, one that went beyond the classroom.

Scene: D Block, Amity College

It was a sunny afternoon, and the trio found themselves in their usual spot at the D Block café. The outdoor seating area was bustling with students, all enjoying a brief respite between classes. The smell of freshly brewed coffee mingled with the laughter and chatter that filled the air.

Yash: (Leaning back in his chair, relaxed) "I have to say, I didn't expect the debate to be that intense. But we handled it pretty well."

Anushka: (Smiling) "We made a good team. Arjun, you really surprised everyone. I think even

Ishika was taken aback."

Arjun: (Shrugging modestly) "It was just a debate. I didn't think much about it."

Yash: (Grinning) "Don't be so humble. You were great. And it was nice to see Ishika taken down a peg."

Anushka chuckled, nodding in agreement. She had noticed the subtle shifts in the dynamics within their class since the debate. Ishika had been quieter and more thoughtful, as if re-evaluating her opinions and perhaps her perceptions of Arjun.

Anushka: (Playfully) "I think you've made an impression, Arjun. You're not just the quiet guy anymore."

Arjun: (Laughing) "I guess that's a good thing?"

Yash: (Teasing) "Definitely. But don't get too used to the spotlight. We like our humble Arjun."

As they continued to chat, the conversation flowed effortlessly, with laughter punctuating their words. It was clear that the bond between them had grown stronger. They supported each other, shared their thoughts openly, and found comfort in each other's company.

Scene: Classroom, Raina Madam's Lecture

A few days later, the trio was back in class, attending Raina Madam's lecture. The room was filled with the quiet hum of students taking notes as Raina Madam spoke, her voice commanding yet engaging.

Raina Madam: (Explaining a concept) "Intelligence isn't just about knowing the right answers. It's about understanding the questions and thinking critically about the solutions."

As she continued her lecture, her gaze swept across the room, pausing briefly on Arjun. She had been observing him for a while now, noting his thoughtful contributions to the class discussions. There was something different about him, an intelligence that was quiet but profound.

Raina Madam: (Pausing) "Arjun, what's your take on this?"

The class turned to look at Arjun, who sat up a little straighter, surprised to be called upon.

Arjun: (Thoughtfully) "I think intelligence also involves empathy, understanding different perspectives and how they impact the solutions we propose. It's not just about logic, but about connecting with the human aspect of every problem."

Raina Madam smiled, clearly impressed.

Raina Madam: (Nodding) "Well said, Arjun. Intelligence without empathy is incomplete. It's good to see you thinking beyond the obvious."

The class murmured in agreement, and Arjun's reputation as more than just a quiet student was further solidified. But it wasn't just Raina Madam who had noticed him; another pair of eyes had been watching him closely.

Raina Madam: (continuing the class) "Today, I want to hear your thoughts on religious tolerance in India. It's a topic that has always been relevant, but especially now, given the current climate. Who would like to start?"

A few students exchanged glances, unsure who would take the lead. After a moment, **Vidhi**, known for her thoughtful opinions, raised her hand.

Vidhi, speaking with quiet conviction: "India has always been known for its diversity. And I think that's one of the greatest things about this country. Hinduism, for example, is a religion that has never been about forcing beliefs on others. It's modern in the sense that it allows freedom, freedom to worship in your own way, to question, and to seek your own path."

Her words were met with nods of agreement from several students, but **Zulfi**, sitting toward the back, folded his arms. His eyes narrowed slightly, and it was clear he wasn't buying into what was being said. **Zulfi** was a hardliner, influenced by the more extreme ideologies in his community. Born and raised in a conservative Muslim household in Uttar Pradesh, he had always been surrounded by narratives that painted India as intolerant toward Muslims.

Zulfi, leaning forward, his voice edged with bitterness: "That's all well and good when you're part of the majority. But as a Muslim in this country, I don't feel the same. There's always a sense of being an outsider. The so-called tolerance is selective, and we're the ones who always have to prove our loyalty."

The tension in the room thickened as **Zulfi's** words hung in the air. **Keshav**, a proud Hindu with a fierce sense of nationalism, straightened in his chair. He had been waiting for this moment, and now he was ready to counter.

Keshav, his voice firm: "Zulfi, that's not fair. India is the most tolerant country in the world. Where else can so many religions coexist so freely? Hinduism has never forced anyone to convert. We've always welcomed other faiths and given refuge to those who needed it. You're talking about discrimination, but look at history; Hindus have always been the first to open their doors to everyone."

The room was charged now, the air thick with unspoken emotions. **Arya**, always the joker, couldn't resist adding a light-hearted comment, though his timing was questionable.

Arya, with a smirk: "Well, if everyone just meditated a little more, maybe we'd all get along."

A few students laughed, but the humour fell flat against the backdrop of the serious conversation. **Raina Madam** shot him a look, and he sank back into his chair, still grinning.

Alisha, a modern Muslim woman who had grown up in a more progressive environment, shook her head slightly. She had listened to **Zulfi's** comments, but she didn't agree with his perspective.

Alisha, her voice measured: "Zulfi, I understand where you're coming from. But I don't think it's entirely fair to paint India as intolerant. I've never felt like an outsider here. In fact, I think our country's strength lies in its ability to embrace differences. Yes, we have issues, but it's not black and white. You can't blame an entire nation for the actions of a few."

Zulfi, his tone sharp: "Easy for you to say, Alisha. You live in a more liberal bubble. You've never faced the kind of prejudice that I have."

Alisha, calmly: "That's not true. I've faced prejudice, but I also know that it's not the norm. People like you, who constantly play the victim card, only add to the divide."

Keshav, his eyes narrowing, added fuel to the fire: "Exactly. India is tolerant, but it's people like you, **Zulfi**, who keep stirring up resentment. You keep talking about oppression, but look around; everyone has the same opportunities here. The problem isn't the country; it's your mindset."

The atmosphere had become charged, almost dangerously so. **Raina Madam**, sensing the tension escalating, tried to mediate.

Raina Madam, gently: "Let's keep this respectful, everyone. We're here to discuss, not attack each other."

But **Zulfi** wasn't done. He leaned forward, invoking a more global issue.
Zulfi, his voice bitter: "What about Palestine? What about Muslims around the world being oppressed? You think India's any different?"

Keshav, his voice cold: "Don't bring foreign politics into this. India isn't like those places. We've given refuge to Jews, Christians, and even Muslims fleeing persecution. It's because of Hinduism's openness that we have this unity. You can't compare India to the Middle East."

Zulfi, with a sneer: "You think this is unity? It's only because Hindus are in the majority. If the tables were turned, you wouldn't be so smug."

The room fell silent again. The tension between **Zulfi** and **Keshav** was palpable now, their glares locked in a silent battle of wills. Other students sat quietly, unsure how to intervene in a discussion that had spiralled beyond the topic of tolerance into something much deeper and darker.

Finally, **Chandamita**, who had been quiet until now, spoke up in an attempt to diffuse the situation. **Chandamita**, calmly: "We can't let this become about us versus them. India's strength is in its diversity. Yes, there are problems, but we can't fix them by pointing fingers. We have to find common ground."

Her words seemed to calm the room, if only slightly. But the underlying tension remained, a reminder that the issue of religious tolerance in India was far more complicated than anyone wanted to admit.

As **Raina Madam** called an end to the discussion, the students filed out; each lost in their own thoughts. The debate had left a mark on the class, one that wouldn't be forgotten easily.

Scene: Avika's Entry

As the class continued, a new student slipped into the back of the room. Avika had recently transferred from Amity's Mumbai branch, and her arrival had not gone unnoticed. Her choice of short, fashionable dresses and confident demeanour made her the subject of much gossip.

As the lecture ended, students began to gather their things. Avika, however, remained seated, her eyes on Arjun. She had been quietly observing him throughout the class, intrigued by his intelligence and the way he carried himself.

Avika: (To herself) "Interesting..."

The next day, during lunch break, the D Block café was as lively as ever. Arjun, Yash, and Anushka were in their usual spot, discussing their plans for the weekend. But today, they had an unexpected visitor.

Avika: (With a playful smile) "Mind if I join you?"

The trio looked up, surprised to scc Avika standing there, holding a tray with her lunch. Anushka, always friendly, was the first to respond.

Anushka: (Smiling) "Of course, take a seat."

As Avika settled in, the conversation shifted to lighter topics. She was charming, effortlessly steering the conversation and keeping everyone engaged. But it was clear that her attention was focused on Arjun.

Avika: (Casually) "So, Arjun, I heard about the debate. You really made an impression."

Arjun looked at her, slightly taken aback by her directness.

Arjun: (Modestly) "It was a team effort. We all played our part."

Avika: (Teasingly) "Don't be so modest. You're different from the other guys here. It's refreshing."

Anushka and Yash exchanged amused glances, sensing the undercurrent in Avika's words. Arjun, however, remained polite, though he couldn't help but notice the intensity in Avika's gaze.

As the lunch break continued, they chatted about various topics, from college life to the latest movies. Avika fit in effortlessly, though it was clear she had her own agenda. She seemed particularly interested in Arjun, subtly steering the conversation back to him whenever it veered away.

Scene: Ishika's Observation

Across the café, Ishika sat with her friends, but her attention was elsewhere. She had noticed Avika joining Arjun's group and had been watching their interaction with growing unease.

Ishika: (To herself) "What's going on there?"

Her friends were chatting about their weekend plans, but Ishika's focus was on Avika and Arjun. She didn't understand why, but seeing them together stirred something within her, a strange mix of jealousy and curiosity.

As the bell rang, signalling the end of lunch break, Ishika quickly gathered her things, unable to shake the feeling that something was changing. Arjun, the quiet boy who had once barely registered on her radar, was now at the centre of her thoughts.

CHAPTER XI

TANGLED WEB OF EMOTIONS

The air in the classroom was thick with anticipation as Ankita Madam assigned the new project. The assignment was a group task requiring collaboration and creativity, a perfect breeding ground for competition and, perhaps, something more.

Scene: Classroom, D Block

Arjun found himself paired with both Ishika and Avika. As they gathered their materials, there was a palpable tension between the two girls. Avika, ever confident, took the lead in discussing the project, but Ishika wasn't about to be overshadowed.

Ishika: (Calmly) "I think we should start with the research. It's important to have a solid foundation before we move forward."

Avika: (Smirking slightly) "Of course, but let's not forget that presentation matters too. We need to make an impact."

Arjun caught between the two, could sense the undercurrent of rivalry. He tried to focus on the task at hand, but the unspoken tension was hard to ignore.

Arjun: (Diplomatically) "Why don't we divide the work? Ishika, you can handle the research, and Avika, you can take charge of the presentation. I'll help where needed."

Both girls agreed, but the looks they exchanged told a different story. The project became less about the assignment and more about outshining each other, with Arjun inadvertently caught in the middle.

Scene: Ankita Madam's Lecture

The next day, the class was deep into a lecture by Ankita Madam. The topic was complex, requiring full attention, but not everyone was focused. Bhati and Naman, sitting at the back, were whispering and snickering, clearly not interested in the lesson.

Ankita Madam's patience finally wore thin.

Ankita Madam: (Sharply) "Bhati, Naman, if you're not interested in learning, you can leave the class."

The room fell silent as all eyes turned to the back of the room. Bhati and Naman caught off guard, tried to play it cool.

Bhati: (Casually) "We're just discussing the assignment, Madam."

Ankita Madam: (Firmly) "You can discuss it outside. Now, leave."

With a smirk and a shrug, Bhati and Naman stood up and sauntered out, their departure followed by murmurs from the rest of the class. The disruption had broken the flow of the lecture, but Ankita Madam quickly regained control, bringing the students' attention back to the lesson.

Ankita Madam, brushing a strand of hair from her face, turned to the board. "Alright, let's get back to where we were. Today, we're going to touch on something that's increasingly relevant in today's world: **Freedom of Speech vs. Hate Speech.**"

The class shifted in their seats. This was a topic that always stirred up heated opinions. **Arjun**, sitting at the back, perked up. He knew this discussion was going to be intense.

Ankita Madam, her voice sharp: "Who can tell me where we draw the line between free speech and hate speech? Where does one end and the other begin?"

Vidhi raised her hand first. "Free speech is about expressing your opinions, but hate speech... it targets and harms people. It can lead to violence."

Ishika, leaning forward: "But where do we decide what's harmful and what's just an opinion? It's subjective, isn't it?"

The room buzzed with murmurs of agreement.

Arjun, raising his hand, spoke up. "Let's take an example. A few years back, there was a case in Germany where a neo-Nazi group wanted to protest. The courts had to decide if their protest fell under freedom of speech or if it was inciting hate. In the end, they banned the protest because it was clear the group's speech could lead to violence and harm."

The class nodded, appreciating the weight of his example.

Then, out of nowhere, **Arya** chimed in, waving his hand in the air. "Sir, I think we should just ban the internet! That way, no one can say anything bad!"

There was a moment of silence before the entire class burst into laughter. **Arya**, as usual, had managed to lighten the mood with his ridiculous suggestion.

Vidhi, wiping a tear of laughter from her eye: "Arya, we're talking about balance, not shutting down the world!"

Ankita Madam, stifling a smile: "Thank you, Arya, for your... creative suggestion. But let's stay on topic."

Suddenly, the conversation took a serious turn. **Yash**, who had been silent until now, spoke up, his voice measured but firm.

Yash: "The problem is that freedom of speech is a right, but it comes with responsibilities. You can't just say anything you want without consequences. If what you say causes harm—like inciting violence or targeting someone based on their identity—that's hate speech. You can't hide behind free speech to hurt others."

Zaki, sitting across the room, leaned in, his tone challenging: "But who decides what's harmful? Isn't it a slippery slope? If we start banning things just because someone finds them offensive, we'll end up censoring everything."

The air in the room thickened as **Yash** shot back, his tone sharpening.

Yash: "That's the point, Zaki. It's not about banning everything offensive. It's about preventing harm. Words have power. You can't just ignore the fact that hate speech leads to real-world violence."

Zaki, crossing his arms: "But doesn't restricting speech lead to more problems? People need to debate and hear different opinions, even the ones they don't like. Otherwise, how do we learn?"

The two of them were locked in a heated exchange, the rest of the class watching with rapt attention.

Ankita Madam, stepping in before it got too intense: "Alright, let's take a breath. Both sides of the argument are important. It's true that free speech is crucial for open dialogue, but it's also true that speech can cross into dangerous territory when it incites hate."

The tension eased, but the debate had clearly left everyone thinking.

In the background, **Arjun** glanced at **Yash**, a newfound respect for his friend's argument. **Arya**, meanwhile, had slouched back in his chair, clearly still thinking about how banning the internet could solve everything.

As the class shifted to a new topic, the weight of the debate still hung in the air. It wasn't an issue with easy answers, but it was one that needed to be discussed.

Scene: D Block Café, Lunch Break

Later that day, the trio of Arjun, Ishika, and Avika met at the D Block café to finalise their project details. The atmosphere was tense, with Avika and Ishika subtly vying for Arjun's attention.

As they discussed the assignment, Avika leaned in closer to Arjun, her voice softening.

Avika: (Playfully) "You know, Arjun, you're really different from the other guys here. I like that."

Arjun, caught off guard by her sudden shift in tone, smiled awkwardly, unsure of how to respond. Ishika, sitting across from them, noticed the interaction and felt a pang of jealousy she couldn't quite understand.

Before the conversation could go any further, Bhati and his friends entered the café. Their eyes landed on Arjun, and a dangerous glint appeared in Bhati's eyes.

Bhati: (Menacingly) "There you are, Arjun. We've been looking for you."

Without warning, Bhati and his group moved towards Arjun, their intent clear. Avika, sensing the danger, stood up quickly.

Avika: (Concerned) "Arjun, let's go."

But it was too late. Bhati grabbed Arjun by the collar, pulling him to his feet.

Bhati: (Sneering) "You think you're smart, don't you? Time to teach you a lesson."

Arjun struggled to free himself, but the group was too strong. Just as things were about to escalate, Raina Madam, who had been passing by, intervened.

Raina Madam: (Authoritatively) "Stop this right now!"

The sheer force of her voice made Bhati and his friends freeze. She stepped forward, her eyes blazing with anger.

Raina Madam: (Coldly) "If you think you can get away with this, you're sorely mistaken. All of you, to the principal's office, now."

Bhati, realising the seriousness of the situation, released Arjun and stepped back, his bravado quickly fading. Raina Madam's presence had effectively defused the situation, but the damage was done.

Scene: Outside the Principal's Office

The news of the incident spread quickly, and by the time Bhati and his friends were standing outside the principal's office, the entire campus knew what had happened. They were soon suspended, a consequence that left Bhati seething with anger.

As Arjun sat on a nearby bench, catching his breath, Ishika approached him, her expression a mix of concern and something else–something softer.

Ishika: (Gently) "Are you okay?"

Arjun looked up, surprised by the warmth in her voice.

Arjun: (Nodding) "Yeah, I'm fine. Thanks."

There was a brief silence, and then, to Arjun's surprise, Ishika hesitated before speaking again.

Ishika: (Softly) "I was thinking... maybe we could go out sometime. Just the two of us."

Arjun blinked, unsure if he had heard her correctly.

Arjun: (Surprised) "A date?"

Ishika nodded, her cheeks flushing slightly.

Ishika: (Smiling) "Yeah, a date."

Before Arjun could respond, Anushka and Yash arrived after hearing about the incident. Ishika excused herself, leaving Arjun alone with his friends.

Scene: Anushka's Advice

Later that evening, as they sat in the college garden, Arjun shared the day's events with Anushka. He mentioned both Avika's proposal and Ishika's unexpected invitation.

Arjun: (Confused) "I don't know what to do. They're both so different, and I'm not sure what I feel."

Anushka, ever the voice of reason, smiled gently.

Anushka: (Kindly) "Arjun, don't overthink it. Listen to your heart. It'll guide you in the right direction."

Arjun nodded, taking in her words. He knew she was right. In the end, it wasn't about what others thought; it was about what he truly wanted.

CHAPTER XII

AMIDST THE FESTIVE FRENZY

The absence of Bhati and his gang had transformed the campus into a much more vibrant and cheerful place. The tension that once lingered in the air had dissipated, replaced by a renewed sense of camaraderie and excitement. Amity College was alive with the buzz of anticipation, and the students revelled in the freedom to enjoy their college life without fear or intimidation.

Scene: H Block, Amity College

It was a bright afternoon in H Block, the heart of Amity College's social life. The open courtyard was bustling with activity. Students lounged on the steps, some engrossed in conversations, while others enjoyed a quick bite from the nearby cafes. The air was filled with laughter, the clinking of coffee cups, and the distant hum of music.

Today, however, there was something extra in the air, a sense of excitement that was palpable.

In the centre of the courtyard, a group of students was practising a dance routine, their movements synchronised and full of energy. Vidhi and Chandamita, two of the most curious and lively girls on campus, were strolling through the courtyard when they noticed the performance.

Vidhi: (Curious) "Hey, what's going on there? Is that a dance rehearsal?"

Chandamita, equally intrigued, leaned closer to catch a glimpse of the action.

Chandamita: (Nodding) "Looks like it. But why so much practice? Something big must be coming up."

Unable to contain their curiosity, the two girls approached the group, eager to find out more. They tapped one of the dancers on the shoulder, a senior they recognised from the cultural committee.

Vidhi: (Excitedly) "Hey, what's all this about? You guys look like you're gearing up for something huge."

The senior smiled, clearly pleased with the attention.

Senior: (Grinning) "You bet! We've got a massive fest coming up next week. And guess who's going to be the chief guest?"

Vidhi and Chandamita exchanged eager glances, their interest piqued.

Chandamita: (Enthusiastically) "Who? Tell us!"

Senior: (With a dramatic pause) "Varun Dhavan and Sara Ali Khan."

The words hung in the air for a moment, and then Vidhi and Chandamita erupted in excitement.

Vidhi: (Squealing) "No way! Are you serious?"

Senior: (Laughing) "Absolutely! They're coming to judge the dance competition and be part of the festivities. It's going to be epic!"

Vidhi and Chandamita could barely contain their excitement. They quickly thanked the senior and rushed off to spread the news, their minds already racing with plans for the upcoming fest.

Scene: The Classroom Buzz

Within minutes, the news spread like wildfire. By the time Vidhi and Chandamita reached their classroom, everyone was talking about the fest. The atmosphere was electric, with students discussing what they would wear, how they would participate, and, of course, who they would go with.

Arjun was sitting at his desk, going over some notes when he noticed the sudden change in the room's energy. Anushka and Yash, who were seated next to him, looked up as Vidhi and Chandamita burst into the room, their faces flushed with excitement.

Vidhi: (Breathlessly) "Guys, did you hear? Varun Bhavan and Sara Ali Khan are coming to our fest!"

Anushka's eyes widened in surprise while Yash raised an eyebrow, clearly impressed.

Yash: (Grinning) "Wow, that's big news. The fest is going to be amazing."

Arjun, however, was more focused on the fact that the fest meant social events–events where he might have to navigate the growing complexities of his relationships with Ishika and Avika.

Scene: A Choice to Make

As the day progressed, the excitement only grew. During lunch at the D Block café, the conversations were dominated by the upcoming fest. Arjun, Anushka, and Yash found themselves at their usual table, but the atmosphere was different. There was an underlying tension, and it didn't take long for the cause of it to reveal itself.

Avika, with her usual confidence, approached their table, her eyes locked on Arjun.

Avika: (Smiling) "Arjun, are you going to the fest?"

Before Arjun could answer, Ishika, who had been sitting nearby, walked over, her expression calm but with a hint of something more.

Ishika: (Casually) "I was just about to ask Arjun the same thing."

The air between the two girls crackled with unspoken rivalry. Anushka and Yash exchanged uneasy glances, sensing the tension that was quickly building.

Avika: (With a slight edge) "Well, Arjun, who are you going with?"

Arjun hesitated, caught off guard by the sudden confrontation. Before he could respond, Anushka, unable to bear the tension, interjected.

Anushka: (Lightly) "Why don't we all go together? It'll be more fun that way."

But her suggestion did little to ease the situation. Avika, clearly not pleased with the idea of sharing Arjun's attention, turned to him directly.

Avika: (Softly) "I'd really like it if you came with me, Arjun."

Before Arjun could respond, Ishika spoke up, her tone more assertive.

Ishika: (Confidently) "We've known each other for a while now, Arjun. I think we'd have a great time together."

The pressure on Arjun was mounting. Anushka, noticing the growing discomfort, tried once more to diffuse the situation.

Anushka: (Gently) "Come on, guys, it's just a fest. Let's not make a big deal out of it."

But Avika wasn't backing down. She turned to Anushka, her voice tinged with irritation.

Avika: (Sharply) "This isn't about you, Anushka. It's between me and Arjun."

The words hung in the air, and before anyone could react, Anushka, feeling slighted, stood up, her eyes flashing with anger.

Anushka: (Firmly) "Well, maybe it should be about me. Arjun is my friend, too, and I'm not going to stand by and watch you manipulate him."

The tension reached its peak as Avika and Anushka faced off. Arjun, sensing that things were about to spiral out of control, quickly stepped in.

Arjun: (Calmly) "Enough, both of you. This isn't how I want things to be."

He turned to Anushka, his voice gentle.

Arjun: "Anushka, I appreciate you looking out for me, but I can handle this."

Then, he turned to Avika, his tone more measured.

Arjun: "Avika, I don't want to hurt you, but I need you to understand that I'm not interested in any drama."

Avika, hurt by his words, stepped back, her expression hardening.

Avika: (Coldly) "I see. Well, have fun at the fest, Arjun."

Without another word, she turned and walked away, leaving an uncomfortable silence in her wake. Ishika, sensing the opportunity, stepped closer to Arjun, her voice soft.

Ishika: (Gently) "So, will you come with me?"

Arjun looked at her, his mind still reeling from the confrontation. But as he met her gaze, he felt a sense of calm. Ishika was offering him a way out of the mess that had just unfolded, and in that moment, the decision seemed clear.

Arjun: (Nodding) "Yeah, I'll go with you."

Ishika smiled, relief washing over her features. Anushka, meanwhile, remained silent, her own feelings a mix of confusion and disappointment.

Scene: Preparing for the Fest

As the news of Arjun's decision spread, the campus buzzed with excitement. The fest, with its promise of celebrity guests, dance performances, and a night of glamour, was the talk of the college. But for Arjun, it was more than just a social event; it was a step into uncharted territory.

Anushka and Yash, though supportive, couldn't help but feel a little left out. The dynamics between the group had shifted, and they both sensed that things would never quite be the same.

CHAPTER XIII

MOONLIT CONFESSIONS

The evening of the much-anticipated fest had finally arrived. The campus was aglow with lights, the atmosphere electric with excitement. Students were dressed to impress, ready to dance the night away under the stars. But for Arjun, the night was already off to a rocky start.

Scene: Arjun's Apartment

Arjun was running late, rushing to finish some last-minute errands. His thoughts were a whirlwind; he knew Ishika wouldn't be happy about his tardiness. As he hurriedly grabbed his jacket, his phone buzzed with a message from Ishika.

Ishika (Text): "Where are you? You're late, Arjun!"

Arjun winced, knowing that her patience was wearing thin. He quickly sent a reply, trying to keep the situation from escalating.

Arjun (Text): "On my way, Ishika. Just finishing up. Be there in a few minutes."

As he rushed out the door, he couldn't shake the feeling that the night was going to be more complicated than he'd anticipated.

Scene: Ishika's Place

Meanwhile, Ishika was pacing in her living room, dressed in a stunning deep red gown that hugged her figure perfectly. Her hair was naturally flowing, and her face, devoid of any makeup, radiated with a beauty that needed no enhancement. She was naturally stunning, a rare kind of beauty that drew admiration effortlessly. But tonight, her mood was anything but serene. She glanced at her watch, frustration building.

As she waited for Arjun, her irritation grew. When she spotted a bottle of wine on the counter, she grabbed it impulsively. One glass turned into two, and by the time Arjun arrived, she was on the verge of anger, with a slight buzz.

Scene: Arjun Arrives

Arjun pulled up to Ishika's place, taking a deep breath before knocking on her door. When she opened it, he was struck by her beauty. The sight of her in that dress, the way her natural beauty glowed in the soft light, took his breath away. Her unadorned face, the soft waves of her hair, her deep, expressive eyes, she was perfection without even trying.

But before he could compliment her, Ishika's irritation spilt over.

Ishika: (Annoyed) "You're late, Arjun! We're going to miss the opening!"

Arjun could see that she was on edge, her eyes slightly glazed from the alcohol. He knew he had to tread carefully.

Arjun: (Apologetically) "I'm really sorry, Ishika. Got caught up in something. You look... amazing."

Her anger softened slightly at his words, but the tension was still there. She huffed and grabbed her purse, heading out to his car. Arjun followed, trying to keep the mood light.

Scene: The Car Ride

As they drove to the fest, Ishika's earlier frustration began to fade, but she reached into her bag and pulled out a small flask. Arjun glanced at her in surprise as she unscrewed the cap and took a swig.

Arjun: (Concerned) "Ishika, are you sure that's a good idea?"

Ishika shrugged, the alcohol already loosening her inhibitions.

Ishika: (Playfully) "I just need something to take the edge off. Don't worry, I'll be fine."

As she leaned back in her seat, her mood shifted from irritation to something more playful but also unpredictable.

Ishika: (Slurring slightly) "You know, Arjun, you're always so calm... It's kind of annoying sometimes."

Arjun glanced at her again, worried. She was clearly not in her usual state.

Arjun: (Gently) "Let's just focus on having a good time tonight, okay?"

Ishika giggled, a bit out of character, and leaned closer to him, her perfume filling the car. Arjun tried to keep his focus on the road, but her proximity was making it difficult.

Scene: The Fest

They arrived at the fest; the campus transformed into a vibrant party scene. The sound of music, laughter, and excitement filled the air. Arjun parked the car and helped Ishika out, noticing how she swayed slightly as she stepped out.

As they walked towards the venue, they were greeted by their friends. Anushka and Vidhi were already on the dance floor, moving to the beat of the music, while Yash and Ananya cheered them on from the sidelines. Karan and Chandamita watched the scene from a distance, their expressions relaxed.

But Ishika seemed unsettled. The noise, the crowd, and the alcohol in her system were starting to overwhelm her. She tugged at Arjun's arm.

Ishika: (Softly) "It's too much... Can we go somewhere quieter?"

Arjun, sensing her discomfort, nodded.

Arjun: "Let's go to the terrace. It'll be quieter there."

Scene: The Terrace

They made their way up to the terrace, leaving behind the noise and the crowd. The moment they stepped outside, they were greeted by the cool night air and the stunning view of the campus, bathed in moonlight. The chaos of the fest seemed miles away, leaving them in a world of their own.

Ishika leaned against the railing, taking deep breaths as she tried to steady herself. Arjun stood beside her, watching her with concern. But as the silence enveloped them, he found himself unable to look away from her.

In the soft glow of the moon, Ishika looked ethereal. Her long, dark hair cascaded over her shoulders, slightly tousled by the breeze. Her dress clung to her curves, highlighting her every movement. But it was her face that captivated him the most, the way her eyes, now softened by the night, held a depth of emotion that he had never seen before.

Arjun's Thoughts:

How could anyone not fall for her? She's so much more than just beautiful... There's a vulnerability in her eyes tonight, a softness that I've never noticed before. And that smile... even when she's upset, it lights up her entire face. She's perfect. Absolutely perfect.

As he stood there, lost in his thoughts, Ishika turned to him, her expression softening as she caught his gaze.

Ishika: (Gently) "I'm sorry for earlier... I didn't mean to get so angry."

Arjun smiled, shaking his head.

Arjun: (Softly) "It's okay. I understand."

They stood in silence for a moment, the distance between them slowly closing. Ishika looked up at him, her eyes searching his.

Ishika's Thoughts:

He's so different... so kind, so patient. I've never met anyone like him. How did I not see it before? He's the kind of person you want by your side... always.

The space between them seemed to disappear, and Arjun could feel his heart pounding in his chest. His gaze travelled from her eyes to her lips, lingering there for a moment. He wanted to close the gap, to feel the softness of her lips against his, but a thousand thoughts raced through his mind. Would she pull away? Was this really happening?

Ishika, too, felt the tension building between them. Her heart raced as she took a step closer, her body language changing, becoming more open, more vulnerable. She could see the desire in Arjun's eyes, and for the first time, she didn't feel the need to push him away.

They were so close now that Arjun could feel the warmth of her breath on his skin. His mind screamed at him to make a move, to seize the moment that was so clearly presenting itself. And yet, there was a hesitance, a fear of ruining what was already so perfect.

But then, as if by some unspoken agreement, they both leaned in. The world around them seemed to fade away, leaving only the two of them standing under the moonlight.

Their lips met softly at first, a tentative brush as if testing the waters. But the moment their skin touched, something inside Arjun ignited. He deepened the kiss, his hand gently cupping her face, pulling her closer. Ishika responded in kind, her hands finding their way to his chest, her touch sending shivers down his spine.

It was everything Arjun had ever imagined. The kiss was tender yet filled with a passion that he had never experienced before. His thoughts were a whirlwind, a mixture of joy and disbelief.

Arjun's Thoughts:

This is really happening... I'm kissing Ishika. I never thought... I never imagined it would feel like this. She's so soft, so warm... It's like everything I've ever wanted is right here, in this moment.

For Ishika, the kiss was a revelation. She had kissed before, but this was different, this was real. The emotions she felt, the way Arjun's touch made her feel safe and cherished, it was unlike anything she had ever experienced. But as the kiss deepened, a small voice in the back of her mind began to whisper doubts.

Slowly, the realisation of what was happening dawned on her. She was kissing Arjun, the boy she had once dismissed as insignificant, the boy she had barely noticed. And now, here she was, letting her guard down completely. The thought sent a wave of panic through her.

She pulled away abruptly, her breath coming in short gasps. Arjun, confused, looked at her with concern.

Arjun: (Softly) "Ishika, what's wrong?"

Ishika took a step back, her hands trembling slightly. The weight of what they had just shared was overwhelming her, and she couldn't handle it.

Ishika: (Shaking her head) "I... I can't. I'm sorry, Arjun. I... I have to go."

Without waiting for his response, she turned and fled, leaving Arjun standing alone on the terrace, the warmth of her lips still lingering on his.

Scene: Arjun's Reflection

As the door closed behind her, Arjun let out a breath he didn't realise he had been holding. His heart was still racing, the adrenaline of the moment coursing through his veins. But as the reality of what had just happened began to sink in, a smile spread across his face.

He had kissed Ishika. The girl who had once seemed so out of reach, so unattainable, had shared this incredible moment with him. He felt a lightness in his chest, a happiness he hadn't known he was capable of.

But as he stood there, basking in the afterglow of the kiss, he couldn't shake the feeling that something had changed. Ishika's abrupt departure left him with more questions than answers, and he knew that whatever had just happened, it wasn't the end; it was just the beginning of something much more complex.

As he walked back inside, Anushka approached him, her expression curious.

Anushka: (Lightly) "What happened? You look... different."

Arjun smiled, shaking his head.

Arjun: "Nothing, Anushka. Just... a really good night."

But as they walked back to join the others, Arjun knew that the night wasn't just good, it was unforgettable. And whatever came next, he was ready to face it, with or without Ishika.

CHAPTER XIV

THE WEIGHT OF DAWN

The sun cast a warm, golden hue over Amity College, breathing life into the sprawling campus. The early morning light filtered through the trees, dappling the red-bricked buildings that stood as silent sentinels of learning. The campus, known for its world-class infrastructure and vibrant student life, was slowly coming alive with the hustle and bustle of a new day. But for Arjun, the serenity of the morning did little to calm the storm inside him.

Scene: Arjun's Walk to College

Arjun walked through the vast playground, usually teeming with energy. Students were already gathering, some setting up for a casual game of volleyball, others preparing for their morning jog around the track. The air was crisp, carrying with it the scent of freshly cut grass and the distant sound of laughter, a typical morning at Amity, where the possibilities seemed endless.

But today, Arjun was lost in his thoughts. His mind kept replaying the events of the previous night, the kiss, the way Ishika had looked under the moonlight, so effortlessly beautiful. Her natural charm, the way her hair framed her face, and the softness of her lips, all of it lingered in his memory. For him, that kiss had been a moment of truth, a spark that could ignite something profound. But as he walked past the modern library, its glass windows reflecting the early light, he couldn't shake the feeling that Ishika might not feel the same way.

Scene: D Block, Outside the Classroom

Arjun arrived at D Block, where the day's classes were about to begin. The building was alive with activity, with students mingling in the hallways, exchanging notes, and preparing for the day ahead. The atmosphere was charged with a sense of purpose, a collective drive to achieve and excel, and hallmarks of the Amity experience.

He spotted Ishika near the entrance, talking to Vidhi. His heart skipped a beat. He wanted to talk to her, to revisit the magic of last night, but as he approached, he noticed her demeanour. She seemed calm, almost detached, as if nothing extraordinary had happened.

Scene: The Conversation

Summoning his courage, Arjun walked up to her, his heart pounding in his chest.

Arjun: (Nervously) "Ishika, can we talk?"

Ishika turned to face him, her expression neutral, almost distant. She nodded, signalling Vidhi to go ahead without her.

Ishika: (Calmly) "Sure, what's up?"

Arjun hesitated, searching her eyes for any sign that she felt the same way he did. But all he saw was the same casual, relaxed look she always had.

Arjun: (Tentatively) "About last night... I've been thinking a lot about it."

Ishika sighed softly, already sensing where the conversation was heading. She decided to be direct.

Ishika: (Casually) "Look, Arjun, it was just a kiss. It didn't mean anything. We were in the moment, that's all. Let's not make it a bigger deal than it was."

Her words hit Arjun like a punch to the gut. He had built up so much hope around that one moment, only to have it dashed in an instant. He tried to mask his disappointment, but it was clear in the way his shoulders slumped, the light in his eyes dimming.

Arjun: (Quietly) "I see..."

Ishika offered a small smile, trying to ease the tension.

Ishika: (Gently) "You're a great guy, Arjun. I just... I don't see you that way. Let's just be friends, okay?"

Arjun forced a smile, nodding even though his heart was breaking. He couldn't understand how something that had meant so much to him could be so easily dismissed by her.

Arjun: (Faintly) "Yeah, friends. Sure."

With that, Ishika turned and walked away, leaving Arjun standing there, feeling more alone than ever. He watched her disappear into the crowd of students, the reality of the situation sinking in. The vibrant, lively campus around him felt dull, the excitement of the new day lost in the heaviness of his heart.

Scene: The Cafeteria, D Block

Feeling like he needed to escape, Arjun made his way to the cafeteria in D Block. The cafeteria, a popular gathering spot, was buzzing with activity. The aroma of freshly brewed coffee mixed with the chatter of students created a lively atmosphere. But today, none of it registered with Arjun.

He found a quiet corner and sat down, his mind replaying the conversation with Ishika over and over again. The usual comfort of the bustling cafeteria felt distant, almost alien.

Anushka, who had been watching Arjun since the morning, noticed his dejected expression and decided to join him. She knew something was wrong and wanted to be there for him.

Anushka: (Concerned) "Hey, you okay?"

Arjun looked up at her, trying to muster a smile but failing.

Arjun: (Sighing) "Not really... I talked to Ishika."

Anushka's heart sank. She had a feeling she knew how the conversation had gone.

Anushka: (Gently) "What did she say?"

Arjun: (Bitterly) "She said it was just a kiss. That it didn't mean anything."

Anushka frowned, feeling a surge of anger towards Ishika for hurting him. She reached across the table and squeezed his hand.

Anushka: (Softly) "I'm so sorry, Arjun. You deserve better than that."

Arjun shrugged, trying to act like it didn't bother him as much as it did.

Arjun: (Murmuring) "It's fine... I guess I just read too much into it."

Anushka shook her head, feeling a protective instinct rise within her.

Anushka: (Firmly) "No, it's not fine. Your feelings are valid, Arjun. And if she can't see how amazing you are, then that's her loss."

Arjun looked at her, appreciating her support. Anushka had always been there for him, and he was grateful for that.

Arjun: (Softly) "Thanks, Anushka. I don't know what I'd do without you."

Anushka smiled, her heart warming at his words.

Anushka: (Gently) "You'll be okay, Arjun. I promise."

Scene: Bhati's Return

As the day went on, word spread quickly through the campus that Bhati was back. The news was met with mixed reactions. Some were wary, others curious. Bhati had been the centre of so much conflict before his suspension, and now his return was bound to stir things up.

Arjun wasn't sure what to expect when he saw Bhati walking through the halls of H Block. But something was different. Gone was the arrogant swagger, the smug look that had defined Bhati's persona. He seemed subdued, almost humble.

Bhati spotted Arjun near the entrance to the main building and made his way over. Arjun tensed, expecting the worst, but was surprised when Bhati extended his hand.

Bhati: (Sincerely) "Arjun, I wanted to say I'm sorry... for everything. I was wrong."

Arjun blinked, taken aback by the apology. This was not the Bhati he remembered.

Arjun: (Hesitantly) "It's... okay, Bhati."

Bhati nodded, his expression sincere.

Bhati: (Sighing) "I've had some time to think, and I realised I needed to change. I just hope we can move past all that."

Arjun studied him for a moment before nodding.

Arjun: (Softly) "Yeah... we can move on."

As Bhati walked away, Arjun felt a strange sense of closure. It wasn't what he had expected, but maybe things were starting to change for the better.

Scene: Avika's Interest

Later that afternoon, as Arjun made his way across the campus, he noticed Avika talking to Bhati near the main entrance. She was smiling, her body language relaxed and open.

It struck Arjun as odd, given how Avika had always seemed so aloof and uninterested in anyone but herself. But there was no denying it; she was interested in Bhati. Arjun watched them for a moment before turning away, realising that everyone was dealing with their own issues, their own changes.

Scene: Reflections

As the sun began to set over the campus, casting long shadows across the playground and the quiet pathways, Arjun found himself reflecting on the day's events. Amity College, with its blend of tradition and modernity, was a place where students were encouraged to dream big and aim high. But it was also a place where realities hit hard, and where lessons were learned, not just in the classrooms, but in the corridors of experience.

He knew that he couldn't dwell on what had happened with Ishika. He had to move on, to focus on what lay ahead. As he walked through the campus, with its majestic buildings and expansive grounds, he felt a sense of resolve.

Life at Amity College was full of ups and downs, but it was also full of possibilities. And while his heart was still heavy from the events of the day, Arjun knew that he would be okay. He had friends like Anushka, and that was enough to help him find his way through the challenges that lay ahead.

CHAPTER XV

FRACTURED TIES

The weight of recent events hung heavily on Arjun as he walked through the campus. The excitement and energy that usually filled the air at Amity College seemed distant, overshadowed by the turmoil in his heart. Ishika's sudden coldness, after everything they had shared, was like a dark cloud that refused to lift. Her indifference cut deeper than he had expected, and despite his best efforts, he couldn't shake the sadness that had settled in.

Scene: Arjun's Room

Arjun sat on the edge of his bed, staring at the ceiling. The events of the past few days played over and over in his mind: his kiss with Ishika, the way she had dismissed it as nothing, and now her deliberate attempts to avoid him. It was as if all the hope he had once felt had been drained away, leaving only a hollow ache in its place.

His phone buzzed with a message, breaking the silence. It was from Anushka.

Anushka (Text): "Hey, want to talk? I'm here if you need me."

Arjun sighed, grateful for her support. He quickly replied.

Arjun (Text): "Yeah, I could use some company."

Scene: The College Garden

A little while later, Arjun met Anushka in the college garden. The sun was beginning to set, casting a warm, golden light over the neatly manicured lawns and flowerbeds. The garden was a place of peace and reflection, and today, it was exactly what Arjun needed.

Anushka was waiting for him on a bench, her expression soft and understanding. She patted the seat beside her, inviting him to sit.

Anushka: (Gently) "You've been through a lot lately. How are you holding up?"

Arjun shrugged, struggling to put his feelings into words.

Arjun: (Sighing) "I don't know, Anushka. I thought things were going somewhere with Ishika, but now... it's like she doesn't even care."

Anushka nodded, her gaze thoughtful.

Anushka: (Softly) "I'm sorry, Arjun. I know how much you liked her. But maybe this is her way of dealing with her own feelings. People react differently when they're scared or confused."

Arjun looked at her, appreciating her insight. Anushka always had a way of seeing things from a perspective he hadn't considered.

Arjun: (Nodding) "Maybe you're right. It just hurts, you know?"

Anushka reached out and squeezed his hand.

Anushka: (Supportively) "I know it does. But you're strong, Arjun. You'll get through this. And no matter what happens, you've got friends who care about you."

Arjun managed a small smile, her words offering a bit of comfort.

Arjun: (Gratefully) "Thanks, Anushka. I don't know what I'd do without you."

Scene: Bhati's Invitation

Later that evening, as Arjun was preparing to head back to his room, his phone buzzed with a call from Bhati. He hesitated for a moment before answering.

Bhati: (On the phone, casually) "Hey, Arjun! Listen, I'm having a party at my farmhouse this weekend. It's going to be a blast. You should come."

Arjun was surprised by the invitation. After everything that had happened between them, he hadn't expected Bhati to reach out.

Arjun: (Hesitantly) "I don't know, Bhati... I'm not really in the mood for a party."

Bhati: (Encouragingly) "Come on, man. It'll be good for you. Get your mind off things. Everyone's going to be there, and it wouldn't be the same without you."

Arjun considered the offer. Part of him wanted to decline, to stay in his room and wallow in his thoughts. But another part of him—perhaps the part that wanted to prove he wasn't as broken as he felt—was tempted to go.

Arjun: (Reluctantly) "Alright, I'll think about it."

Bhati: (Cheerfully) "Great! I'll send you the details. See you there!"

After hanging up, Arjun found himself conflicted. The idea of going to a party, especially one hosted by Bhati, was far from appealing. But before he could dwell on it, Yash appeared, having overheard the conversation.

Scene: Yash's Advice

Yash: (Concerned) "You're not seriously thinking about going, are you?"

Arjun looked at his friend, knowing Yash had his best interests at heart.

Arjun: (Sighing) "I don't know, Yash. Maybe it'll help take my mind off things."

Yash shook his head, clearly not convinced.

Yash: (Firmly) "I get that you want a distraction, but Bhati's parties are trouble. You don't need to get mixed up in that right now."

Arjun knew Yash was right, but something in him pushed back against the advice.

Arjun: (Resolutely) "I appreciate the concern, Yash, but maybe I need this. I can't just sit around feeling sorry for myself."

Yash sighed, recognising the determination in Arjun's voice.

Yash: (Gently) "Just be careful, okay? If things get out of hand, don't hesitate to leave."

Arjun nodded, grateful for his friend's concern.

Arjun: (Reassuringly) "I will. Don't worry."

Scene: The Farmhouse Party

When the weekend arrived, Arjun found himself standing in front of Bhati's sprawling farmhouse. The place was impressive, luxurious and tastefully decorated, with a large garden and a pool that glimmered under the evening lights. The sound of music and laughter drifted from inside, mingling with the warm night air.

As he stepped inside, he was greeted by the sight of his college peers, all dressed to impress, dancing, chatting, and enjoying the night. Bhati spotted him from across the room and made his way over.

Bhati: (Grinning) "Glad you could make it, Arjun! Enjoy yourself; this night's about forgetting all our worries."

Arjun nodded, trying to relax. He grabbed a drink and wandered around the party, trying to get into the festive spirit. But despite the lively atmosphere, his thoughts kept drifting back to Ishika.

It wasn't long before he spotted her. She was standing by the pool, talking to some friends, looking as effortlessly beautiful as ever. But tonight, he was determined not to let her get to him. He turned away, deliberately avoiding her gaze.

Scene: Ishika's Attempt

Ishika, however, had noticed Arjun the moment he walked in. She had been hoping to talk to him, to explain herself, but she could see the coldness in his demeanour. He wasn't going to make it easy for her.

Summoning her courage, she approached him as he stood by the bar, sipping his drink.

Ishika: (Softly) "Arjun... can we talk?"

Arjun glanced at her, his expression unreadable.

Arjun: (Coldly) "What's there to talk about?"

Ishika felt a pang of guilt at his tone but pressed on.

Ishika: (Apologetically) "About everything... I know I hurt you, and I'm sorry. I didn't mean to."

Arjun shrugged, his voice distant.

Arjun: (Flatly) "It's fine, Ishika. You made yourself clear. Let's just leave it at that."

She could see the hurt in his eyes, even though he was trying to hide it. But before she could say anything more, Arjun turned and walked away, leaving her standing there, feeling more alone than ever.

Scene: Ups and Downs

As the night went on, the tension between Arjun and Ishika only grew. They danced around each other, both trying to avoid the pain that lingered between them. Arjun threw himself into the party, trying to forget, while Ishika found herself watching him from a distance, regretting the choices that had led them here.

It was a night of ups and downs, of moments where they almost crossed paths only to pull back at the last second. Both of them were lost in their own emotions, unsure of how to bridge the growing gap between them.

As the party wound down and the guests began to leave, Arjun found himself outside, staring up at the stars. The night had been a blur, and now, standing alone in the quiet, he couldn't help but feel the weight of it all.

Ishika, too, stood alone, watching him from afar. She wanted to reach out, to make things right, but she didn't know how. And so, they remained apart, both of them wishing for something different yct unable to find the words to make it happen.

As the night ended, they went their separate ways, the distance between them wider than ever. But deep down, both of them knew that this wasn't the end; there was still more to their story, more that needed to be said, more that needed to be felt.

The night had been just another chapter in their complicated journey, one filled with twists and turns, and neither of them knew what the next day would bring.

CHAPTER XVI

A DANCE OF EMOTIONS

The days following the party at Bhati's farmhouse had been a whirlwind of emotions for **Arjun**. **Ishika's** aloofness had left him feeling hollow, and despite **Anushka's** efforts to cheer him up, he couldn't shake the growing ache in his chest. He would often catch glimpses of **Ishika** around campus, but their interactions had dwindled to cold glances and fleeting moments that left him more frustrated than ever.

He had tried to move on, pushing his focus back to his classes and sports, but his heart was stubborn. No matter how hard he tried, his mind kept wandering back to that kiss, the way their lips had met so naturally, the warmth that had blossomed in his chest, and the hope that had flickered alive. Yet, it was all confusingly tangled in her sudden distance afterwards. She was no longer the radiant girl who had kissed him on the terrace but someone far more complex, unreachable.

The final blow came when **Anushka**, with a soft expression that spoke volumes, told him about

Ishika's upcoming birthday. It seemed the entire class was invited, and for **Arjun**, it felt like fate was dangling another chance in front of him, a chance to change things between them.

It started with a casual mention in the cafeteria, one of **Ishika's** friends enthusiastically chatting about the grand birthday celebration Ishika's family was planning at their home in New Friends Colony. The mention of her birthday sent a ripple of excitement through the campus, and soon, it was all anyone could talk about. **Ishika Kapoor's** birthday was an event, and it was no surprise, given who she was: a princess-like figure whose presence alone could enchant an entire room.

Anushka: "Are you going?" she had asked casually, though her eyes were watchful. "Everyone's talking about it. I heard it's going to be pretty extravagant."

Arjun hesitated. He had been avoiding events where **Ishika** would be present, fearing it would only lead to more heartbreak. But something about this felt different. It felt like an opportunity he couldn't pass up.

Arjun: "Yeah, I think I'll go," he finally said, though his voice was distant, as if he was convincing himself more than anything.

Anushka gave him a long, considering look but said nothing. She could sense there was more behind his decision, but she didn't press. In her heart, she knew how much **Arjun** still cared about **Ishika**, even if he hadn't fully admitted it to himself.

As the days inched closer to the party, **Arjun** found himself faced with a new dilemma: what would he get her? A simple gift wouldn't do; it had to be something meaningful. Something that would show her he understood her, even if she was pushing him away. The choice weighed heavily on him, but after wandering through several shops, he found a delicate silver necklace with a tiny diamond pendant, a piece of elegance that mirrored **Ishika's** own understated grace.

The Night of the Party

The night of **Ishika's** birthday arrived sooner than expected, and as **Arjun** stepped out of his car in front of her grand house in New Friends Colony, a wave of nerves washed over him. Her house was breathtaking, illuminated by soft lights and surrounded by an aura of elegance. It was a palace fit for royalty, and tonight, **Ishika** was the queen.

Arjun wasn't sure what to expect when he walked in, but the moment he entered the house, the air shifted. The music was soft, the decor tasteful, and the guests mingled with a sense of ease, but his eyes immediately searched for **Ishika**, his pulse quickening with every passing second.

And then, he saw her.

Ishika stood at the centre of the room; her back turned to him at first. But even from this angle, she was mesmerising. She wore a black gown that hugged her curves elegantly, the fabric shimmering under the lights. Her long, dark hair cascaded down her back in soft waves, brushing gently against her bare shoulders. And when she turned around, it was as if time itself had stopped.

Her beauty was heart-stopping. **Arjun** felt his breath catch as he took in her appearance; her face was completely devoid of makeup, yet it was flawless. Her skin glowed with a natural radiance, and her eyes, deep and dark, sparkled like stars. Her lips, soft and full, looked as if they had been painted by an artist's brush, their colour natural yet striking. And her cheeks—slightly flushed—held the warmth of a setting sun, softening her face and drawing attention to her elegance.

She wore no jewellery except for a single diamond bracelet on her wrist, a simple yet stunning piece that seemed to twinkle with every movement she made. There was something so unassuming about her, and yet she carried herself like royalty. **Arjun** couldn't help but think of her as a princess, an ethereal figure that no one could take their eyes off of.

His heart raced. She was the most beautiful woman he had ever seen, and at that moment, he knew with absolute certainty that he was in love with her. It wasn't just the kiss or the way she looked tonight; it was everything about her. The way she held herself with quiet confidence, the vulnerability she tried so hard to hide, the glimpses of warmth and softness that peeked through when she thought no one was watching. She was complicated and challenging, but **Arjun** found himself wanting to unravel every layer of her.

As he approached her, his nerves fluttered, but he was determined. Tonight, he would tell her how he felt, no matter what.

But before he could reach her, someone else caught his attention. A woman was standing beside **Ishika**, laughing softly as they spoke. She was older than **Ishika** but bore a striking resemblance to her, with the same eyes and the same graceful features. **Arjun** realised this must be **Ishika's sister**.

Sanya, smiling warmly: "Hi, you must be Arjun. I'm Sanya, Ishika's sister. She's mentioned you."

Arjun, nervous: "Nice to meet you."

Sanya, with a knowing look: "You're the one who's been occupying her thoughts lately, aren't you?"

Arjun blushed, but **Sanya** laughed softly.

Sanya: "Don't worry, Arjun. Ishika's not as tough as she seems. She's just... complicated."

Arjun, curious: "Complicated how?"

Sanya glanced at **Ishika**, who was now talking to some friends across the room.

Sanya, quietly: "She's had a tough childhood. Our parents weren't the most... supportive. They always expected perfection from her, and she's spent her whole life trying to meet those expectations. It's left her guarded, afraid to let people in."

Hearing this softened **Arjun's** heart. He approached **Ishika** and asked her for a dance.

Arjun: "Would you like to dance?"

Ishika, surprised at first, smiled. "Yes."

As they moved to the centre of the room, the music shifted to a slow, romantic melody. **Arjun** placed his hand on the small of her back, pulling her closer, and they began to sway to the music. The world around them faded away, and it was just the two of them moving together in perfect harmony.

Arjun looked down at her, his heart full. He could feel the softness of her skin, the warmth of her breath against his neck, the gentle beat of her heart as they danced. She was everything he had ever wanted and more.

Around them, people watched, whispering softly to each other, but neither **Arjun** nor **Ishika** paid them any attention. For the first time in a long while, **Ishika** let herself relax in **Arjun's** arms. She wasn't thinking about expectations or perfection–she was just here, with him.

And as they danced, **Arjun** knew that this was the moment he had been waiting for. Tomorrow, he would tell her everything. He would confess his feelings, lay his heart bare, and hope that she felt the same.

But for now, he was content to just hold her close, savouring the feel of her in his arms.

After the party had ended, **Arjun** found **Anushka** waiting for him outside, her expression unreadable.

Anushka, quietly: "How was it?"

Arjun smiled, his heart still full from the dance.

Arjun, softly: "It was perfect. I'm going to tell her tomorrow. I'm going to tell her I'm in love with her."

Anushka remained silent for a moment, her eyes distant, as if she was wrestling with her own thoughts. And then, finally, she nodded, though her smile was faint.

Anushka, whispering: "Good luck."

There was a sadness in her voice that **Arjun** couldn't quite place.

As he walked away, **Arjun** couldn't help but feel a sense of anticipation. Tomorrow, everything will change. Tomorrow, he would tell **Ishika** how he truly felt.

And for the first time in a long time, he felt hopeful.

CHAPTER XVII

THE COST OF SILENCE

As the night of Ishika's birthday passed, Arjun couldn't stop replaying the moments in his mind, dancing with her, the way she had looked at him with a softness he hadn't seen before. He was on the verge of something monumental, a shift in his feelings that was both exhilarating and terrifying. And now, with his emotions clear, he was ready to confess his love to Ishika, the woman who had somehow found her way into his heart.

The next day, Arjun found himself sitting in the college garden with Anushka. She had noticed the way he had been acting since the party and knew something was up. But there was something in her expression today–a quiet sadness that she couldn't quite hide.

Anushka: (Concerned) "Arjun, are you sure about this? I know you're planning to talk to Ishika, but I can't help but feel...worried."

Arjun: (Softly) "Why? I've never been this sure about anything in my life, Anushka. I feel like we've been through so much, and now, it just feels right. I'm going to tell her how I feel."

Anushka: (Sighing) "I get that. But what about everything that's happened between you two? Ishika has made mistakes, and she's hurt you before. What if this doesn't go the way you're hoping?"

Arjun hesitated for a moment, his thoughts wandering back to the ups and downs between him and Ishika. The arguments, the misunderstandings, and the way she had dismissed him after their kiss. But despite everything, something in his heart told him that this time would be different.

Arjun: (Thoughtfully) "Yeah, she has hurt me. I know that. There were times when I couldn't understand her and felt like she was just pushing me away. After the kiss, I was crushed. It felt like I'd misread everything, and I was ready to give up on her. But last night...something changed. I saw a different side of her, Anushka. I saw the real Ishika, and I think she's just scared."

Anushka: (Gently) "Scared of what, Arjun? You can't ignore the fact that she's been cold to you before. What if she does it again? I don't want to see you hurt."

Arjun: (Firmly) "I know, and I appreciate that you're looking out for me. But I think she's afraid to be vulnerable. Last night, when we talked...she told me about her childhood, her family, and all the pressure she's been under. I think she's just been protecting herself. Maybe she's never felt real love before."

Anushka looked at him, her concern deepening. She could see that Arjun was convinced that Ishika had changed, but she couldn't shake the feeling that this could end badly. Still, she knew he had to follow his heart, even if it meant taking the risk.

Anushka: (Softly) "I just don't want you to get hurt again, Arjun. But if this is what you really want...then I'll support you. Just be careful, okay?"

Arjun smiled at her, grateful for her support. He didn't notice that Ishika had overheard part of their conversation just a few feet away, hidden by a nearby tree. But she hadn't heard everything, only the part where Arjun had mentioned her mistakes and how she had hurt him. Her heart sank as she misunderstood his words, thinking that Arjun was only focused on the bad parts of their relationship, that perhaps he was using her as some kind of emotional rebound.

Ishika's mind raced with doubt and anger. Had she been wrong about him? Was Arjun just playing with her emotions, only seeing her faults and not caring about who she really was? The thoughts spiralled in her head, and before she knew it, she was storming over to where Arjun and Anushka were sitting.

Ishika: (Furious) "What the hell, Arjun? So all you think about is how I hurt you? That's all I am to you, right? A mistake?"

Arjun looked up, startled. He stood quickly, trying to figure out what had happened.

Arjun: (Confused) "Ishika, wait, what are you talking about?"

Ishika: (Angry, tears in her eyes) "I heard what you said! You've been going on about how I've hurt you, how I've made mistakes. Is that what all this was to you? A game to make me feel guilty?"

Arjun: (Desperately) "No, that's not what I meant at all. You didn't hear everything–"

But Ishika was too upset to listen. Her insecurities and fears had taken over, and she wasn't in a state to hear him out.

Ishika: (Coldly) "Don't bother explaining, Arjun. I've had enough. I don't need you to make me feel worse about myself. Just...fuck off. Don't ever talk to me again."

Her words were sharp, cutting through Arjun like a knife. He stood there, stunned, as Ishika turned on her heel and walked away, her shoulders shaking with anger and hurt. Arjun wanted to go after her, to explain everything, but he could already tell that the damage was done.

Anushka: (Gently) "Arjun..."

Arjun shook his head, unable to speak. The ache in his chest was overwhelming. He had been so close to telling Ishika how he felt, to showing her the love he had been holding back. But now, it was all crumbling before him, and he didn't know how to fix it.

Anushka placed a comforting hand on his shoulder, but Arjun barely noticed. His mind was spinning, trying to make sense of what had just happened.

Scene: Exams and End of the Year

The days that followed were a blur for Arjun. The end of the academic year was fast approaching, and everyone was busy preparing for their final exams. The campus, once vibrant and alive with social activity, had turned into a place of quiet concentration as students buried themselves in their studies.

But for Arjun, it was hard to focus. Every time he tried to study, his mind drifted back to Ishika, her anger, her hurt, and the way she had looked at him before she walked away. He couldn't get her out of his head, no matter how hard he tried.

Ishika, too, had thrown herself into her studies, avoiding any interaction with Arjun. She kept her distance, refusing to give him the chance to explain himself. It was easier that way to keep him at arm's length, to convince herself that she was better off without him.

Their friends noticed the tension but didn't push either of them. It was clear that something had gone wrong between Arjun and Ishika, but no one wanted to get involved. They all had their own exams to worry about and their own futures to focus on.

Scene: Raina Madam's Office

One afternoon, Arjun found himself sitting in Raina Madam's office. She had called him in for a meeting, sensing that something was off with one of her brightest students.

Raina Madam: (Kindly) "Arjun, I've noticed you've been a bit distracted lately. Is everything okay?"

Arjun sighed, running a hand through his hair. He didn't know where to begin.

Arjun: (Tiredly) "It's just...a lot has happened. I've been trying to figure things out with Ishika, but it's all gone wrong. And now, with exams coming up, I feel like everything is slipping away."

Raina Madam listened carefully, her expression softening. She had always seen potential in Arjun, but she knew that life outside the classroom could sometimes be just as challenging as the academic pressures.

Raina Madam: (Gently) "Arjun, I know things with Ishika are complicated. But you have to remember what's most important right now, your future. You've worked hard to get here, and you can't let personal issues get in the way of your career. Focus on what you can control. The rest...will work itself out in time."

Arjun nodded, understanding what she was saying. But the weight of his feelings for Ishika still hung heavy on his heart.

Raina Madam: (Encouragingly) "I know it's hard, but you're stronger than you think, Arjun. You have the potential to do great things. Don't lose sight of that because of one setback."

Arjun looked up at her, grateful for her words. He knew she was right. He couldn't let this break him. There was too much at stake, too much to lose if he didn't pull himself together.

Arjun: (Resolutely) "Thank you, ma'am. I'll do my best."

Raina Madam smiled, giving him a reassuring nod.

Raina Madam: (Softly) "I know you will. Now go, get back to studying. You have a bright future ahead of you, Arjun. Don't let anyone take that away from you."

As Arjun left her office, he felt a renewed sense of determination. He couldn't change what had happened with Ishika, but he could control his future. And for now, that had to be enough.

Interlude: The End of Innocence

The second year at Amity College had come to an end, leaving behind a trail of memories, some cherished, some painful. The campus, once a haven of excitement and endless possibilities, now held the weight of lessons learned, friendships tested, and hearts broken.

Arjun had entered the year with hope in his heart, eager to find his place in the ever-shifting social landscape of college life. But as the year unfolded, so did the complexities of relationships and the harsh realities of growing up. The thrill of first love had been tempered by misunderstandings and heartbreak, leaving Arjun to navigate the emotional fallout on his own.

Ishika had come into his life like a whirlwind, drawing him into her world with her beauty, charm, and mystery. But just as quickly, that world had been shattered by a few misunderstood words, leaving both of them to pick up the pieces in their own way. The connection they had once shared now felt fragile, and the distance between them seemed insurmountable.

Anushka, his steadfast friend and confidante, had been a constant source of support through it all. But now, even she was moving on, transferring to the Dubai branch, leaving Arjun to face the challenges of the third year without her by his side. Yash, too, had become distant, his focus shifting to his studies and career, leaving little time for the camaraderie they once enjoyed.

As the summer heat settled over the sprawling campus, the atmosphere grew quieter and more reflective. The laughter and energy that had once filled the corridors of H Block had faded, replaced by the quiet determination of students preparing for their final exams. The end of the second year marked a turning point, a time to reflect on the past and prepare for the future.

For Arjun, the year had been one of transformation. He had come to understand the complexities of love, the pain of rejection, and the importance of resilience. He had learned that not every story ends in the way you hope, but that doesn't mean it isn't worth telling.

But as one chapter closed, another was just beginning. The third year promised new challenges, new friendships, and new opportunities. The mistakes of the past would serve as lessons, guiding Arjun as he stepped into this next phase of his journey. There would be no more innocence, no more naivety, only the hard-won wisdom that comes from experience.

The future was uncertain, but it was also full of possibilities. And as Arjun looked ahead, he knew that, no matter what, he was ready to face whatever came next. The third year would be a time of new beginnings and, perhaps, just maybe, the start of something truly extraordinary.

CHAPTER XVIII

PATHS CONVERGE

The third year had just begun, but it felt like everything was slipping away for Arjun. The bustling corridors of Amity College once filled with energy and excitement, now felt strangely quiet. He walked slowly towards class, barely noticing the students rushing past him.

Anushka was transferring to the Dubai branch. As Anushka's departure neared, the reality of her leaving began to sink in for Arjun. Her father, a former police officer, had left his job and started a business in Dubai, prompting her family's move. One evening, Arjun, Anushka, and Yash sat together at their usual spot in H Block, the air filled with a mix of nostalgia and sadness.

Anushka: *"I can't believe it's really happening... I'll be in Dubai in a few days."*

Her voice was calm but carried a weight that reflected the enormity of the change.

Yash: *"It feels strange, doesn't it? Like, after all we've been through, this is how it ends."*

Arjun: *"You've been such a big part of my life here. I don't know how it's going to be without you."*

Anushka smiled softly, her eyes reflecting the emotion of the moment.

Anushka: *"I'll miss you guys too. But you know this isn't goodbye forever, right? I'll be just a call away."*

Yash nodded, trying to lighten the mood.

Yash: *"You better visit us when you're back. And we'll try to come see you in Dubai."*

They laughed, but the sadness lingered. When it was time to say goodbye, Arjun hugged Anushka tightly. The tears he had been holding back threatened to spill over, and his voice cracked.

Arjun: *"I'm really going to miss you, Anushka."*

Anushka held on for a moment longer, her voice gentle.

Anushka: *"We'll be okay, Arjun. You'll always be my friend, no matter where we are."*

As they finally parted, Yash joined them in one last group hug. The three of them stood together, holding on to the promise that, despite the distance, their friendship would remain.

In the classroom, Raina Madam was addressing the students.

Raina Madam: *"Good morning, everyone! Welcome to your third year. You've made it this far, and I expect each of you to push yourselves even harder this year. The future is bright for those who seize it."*

Raina Madam, known for her thought-provoking discussions, stood at the front, her expression serious but inviting.

Raina Madam: "Alright, everyone. Before we dive into today's session, I'd like to get your thoughts on something that's been dominating the news lately: **CAA and NRC**. I know it's a sensitive topic, but as educated individuals, it's important that we understand all perspectives. So, what do you think? Let's keep it civil."

A murmur spread across the class. Some students exchanged uneasy glances while others leaned forward, ready to jump into the debate.

Luqman, always vocal and passionate about societal issues, was the first to speak.

Luqman, invoking a religious angle: "It's clear this law is designed to target Muslims. How can we ignore the religious divide it creates? Muslims are being left out deliberately, and no one is addressing that."

Across the room, **Keshav**, a proud Hindu, shook his head, clearly agitated.

Keshav, his voice clipped but controlled: "This isn't about religion, Luqman. It's about giving refuge to persecuted minorities from neighbouring countries. People who've faced atrocities. How can we turn our backs on them?"

Zulfi, leaning forward, his tone more heated: "So, you're saying Muslims don't face persecution? What about the Rohingya in Myanmar or the Uighurs in China? Why aren't they included? This law is clearly selective and dangerous."

The tension in the room ratcheted up a notch as more students started murmuring in low tones. The debate had touched a nerve, and it was clear that the discussion was treading on sensitive ground.

Keshav firmly said: "The law is about helping those who have no other place to go, Zulfi. It's not an anti-Muslim agenda. Indian Muslims are not affected by this. You're twisting the issue into something it's not."

Zulfi, eyes narrowing: "That's easy to say when your community isn't the one being questioned, isn't it? The **NRC** will lead to harassment; people will be forced to prove their citizenship in a way they never had before. It's a systematic way of excluding us."

The atmosphere in the room became taut, the air almost electric. Eyes darted nervously around as the debate grew more pointed. The room was split, some nodding along with **Keshav**, others quietly supporting **Zulfi** and **Luqman**.

Raina Madam, sensing the charged energy, raised her hand slightly, signalling for the class to calm down, but the undercurrent of tension lingered, making it clear that this was a discussion far from over.

Zulfi, his tone sharp: "Keshav, you're ignoring the reality. The **NRC** is just a tool to target us. How can you support something that will put millions of Muslims through hell, forcing them to prove their citizenship while others get a free pass?"

Keshav, leaning forward, his voice steady but firm: "Zulfi, the **NRC** is about national security. It's not about targeting anyone. We need to know who's in the country, who's legal and who's not. It applies to everyone, not just Muslims. You're blowing this out of proportion."

Zulfi, voice rising: "Blowing it out of proportion? Do you think it's a coincidence that only Muslims will face the consequences? It's clear this law is discriminatory. First the **CAA**, now the **NRC**–it's like they're building a wall around us."

Keshav, not backing down: "And what's the alternative? Let anyone walk in without checks? Every country has a system to protect its borders. This isn't some anti-Muslim conspiracy; it's basic governance."

Zulfi, his eyes narrowing: "Basic governance? When only one community is being targeted, that's not governance; that's oppression. The government is using fear to divide us, and you're falling for it."

The class was completely silent now, the air thick with tension. Both **Zulfi** and **Keshav** sat rigid, their words cutting through the stillness like a knife.

Keshav, his voice low but sharp: "Fear? The only fear I see is the one being stoked by people who refuse to see reason. This isn't about religion. This is about keeping the country safe."

Zulfi, leaning forward, his tone biting: "Safe for whom? People like you, maybe. But for us? We're the ones paying the price for your so-called safety."

The discussion had reached a dangerous pitch, the class frozen between the clashing viewpoints, the tension hanging like a storm ready to break.

Raina Madam, sensing the tension escalating, raised her hand to mediate, her voice calm but firm: "Alright, that's enough. We're here to discuss, not attack one another. Let's keep this respectful."

But **Zulfi** was already leaning forward, eyes blazing. His voice was sharp as he invoked another issue.
Zulfi: "Respect? Is that what you call what's happening in Palestine? You think these laws won't lead us down the same path? One step at a time,

erasing us from our own land?"

Keshav, his tone scathing: "Oh, so now you're comparing India to Palestine? You're justifying violence with your propaganda. You sound like a jihadi more than a student right now."

The class collectively tensed as **Zulfi's** face darkened.
Zulfi, voice seething: "You dare call me that? Just because I'm Muslim? That's exactly the mentality this government is promoting. Label anyone who disagrees with you, turn them into the enemy."

Keshav, standing his ground, eyes cold: "You've already made yourself the enemy with your words. Always playing the victim, turning every issue into a religious fight. The country doesn't need people like you constantly dividing it."

The room was now suffocating with tension. **Raina Madam** stepped in again, her tone more urgent this time.
Raina Madam: "That's enough from both of you. This is not the place for personal attacks. If we can't discuss this respectfully, we'll stop the conversation right here."

But the damage was done. **Zulfi** and **Keshav** locked eyes, the hatred simmering beneath the surface clear for everyone to see. The argument had spiralled beyond the topic, touching on deeper, more personal wounds that no amount of mediation could heal.

Amid all this frenzy, Arjun listened passively, his thoughts elsewhere. Anushka was transferring to the Dubai branch, Yash was distant, too buried in his studies to spend time together, and both Ishika and Avika were out of his life.

After class, Arjun walked to the campus lawn, sitting alone. He watched as groups of friends passed by, laughing and enjoying their time together. For the first time, he felt truly alone. His phone buzzed with a notification: a party invite at Gardens Galleria Mall. On a whim, he decided to go, hoping for a brief distraction from his thoughts.

The party at Gardens Galleria was in full swing by the time Arjun arrived. Music pulsed through the venue, and people crowded the dance floor. Arjun found a corner, keeping mostly to himself as he sipped his drink. Just then, a familiar voice called out to him.

Bhati: *"Arjun! I didn't expect to see you here, man!"*

Arjun turned, a bit surprised to see Bhati. For a moment, he considered walking away, but something stopped him.

Arjun: *"Yeah, didn't expect to come. Just needed a break, I guess."*

Bhati smiled, holding up his glass.

Bhati: *"Join me for a drink?"*

Arjun hesitated but then nodded. They moved to a quieter part of the venue, drinks in hand. The conversation started slowly and awkwardly, but Bhati seemed genuinely open.

Bhati: *"You know, I've been meaning to talk to you for a while."*

Arjun: *"Yeah? About what?"*

Bhati took a deep breath before continuing.

Bhati: *"Listen, man, I know I've been a jerk. Maybe more than that. But I've been thinking...maybe I haven't been fair to you."*

Arjun raised an eyebrow, not expecting this turn.

Arjun: *"You're right. You weren't."*

Bhati laughed a bit nervously but nodded.

Bhati: *"Yeah, I deserve that. Look, it's not an excuse, but there's always been pressure. Pressure to be the best, to never show weakness. And sometimes...I let that get to me. I took it out on people, on you."*

Arjun stayed silent for a moment, processing Bhati's words.

Arjun: *"It wasn't just pressure, though. You were harsh for no reason."*

Bhati sighed and looked away for a moment before turning back.

Bhati: *"You're right. And I'm not proud of it. But I've changed, man. I'm trying to be better. These last few months...I've realised a lot. About myself, about how I treat people."*

Arjun watched him carefully, looking for any signs of insincerity. But Bhati's expression was honest, even vulnerable.

Arjun: *"So why the change?"*

Bhati: *"I guess I grew up a little. Life isn't all about showing off or putting others down. People...they matter."*

They sat in silence for a moment, the party continuing around them. Arjun felt something shift inside him; maybe Bhati really had changed.

Bhati: *"What about you, man? You seem...different. What's going on?"*

Arjun leaned back, his drink untouched.

Arjun: *"Everything's changed. Anushka's transferring, Yash is busy all the time, and Ishika...well, she's gone too."*

Bhati nodded sympathetically.

Bhati: *"That's tough, man. But you're not alone, you know? Sometimes, it just takes opening up to the right* *people."*

Arjun looked at Bhati, surprised by the sincerity in his voice. The laughter between Arjun and Bhati was genuine now, the old animosity fading away with each sip of their drinks. It was hard for Arjun to believe how quickly things were changing, but he welcomed it. Just then, Naman and Vicky spotted them from across the room and made their way over.

Naman: *"Arjun, Bhati! What's going on here? Looks like you guys are having a good time!"*

Vicky: *"Mind if we join?"*

Arjun smiled, nodding as they pulled up chairs. It was strange; these were the guys who used to laugh at him and even mock him, but now they seemed different. More respectful, like they had begun to see him in a new light.

Bhati: *"Come on, guys, join us. We were just talking about life, you know, how things change."*

They all laughed, settling into the rhythm of conversation. The awkwardness that used to linger between them was gone. They were just a group of guys hanging out, enjoying each other's company. Soon, they decided that the night was too young to end.

Naman: *"You know what, let's take this party somewhere else. Gardens Galleria is cool, but we need something more... epic."*

Vicky: *"Yeah, let's make this night one to remember."*

Bhati grinned, looking at the group.

Bhati: *"I know just the place. How about Hotel Taj at Chanakyapuri? We can book a suite, and we can really enjoy ourselves."*

Arjun shrugged, ready to go with the flow.

Arjun: *"Why not? Let's do it."*

A short while later, they arrived at the Hotel Taj, Chanakyapuri. As soon as they entered, something surprising happened. The general manager, a tall man dressed in an impeccable suit, spotted Arjun and rushed over, his face lighting up with recognition.

General Manager: *"Mr. Arjun, sir! It's so good to see you again!"*

He greeted Arjun with a bow, shaking his hand warmly. Bhati, Naman, and Vicky exchanged confused glances but said nothing.

General Manager: *"Please, let me take care of everything for you. We'll get the best suite ready right away. And, of course, a bottle of wine and a special platter of buffalo steaks—your favourite."*

Arjun smiled, trying not to look too affected by the attention.

Arjun: *"Thanks, appreciate it."*

The general manager rushed off to make the arrangements, leaving Bhati and the others standing in stunned silence.

Naman: *"Dude... what was that? The manager knew you by name?"*

Vicky: *"And steaks... and wine? You eat steaks, man?"*

Arjun chuckled, looking a bit embarrassed by the whole thing.

Arjun: *"Yeah, I guess I've been here a few times."*

Bhati: *"A few times? They're treating you like a king!"*

Arjun could sense the curiosity building in their voices. They wanted to know more, and truth be told, he was tired of keeping his secrets hidden.

Naman: *"Seriously, man. How do you pull off tricks like this? You always seemed like a simple guy, but clearly, there's more to you."*

Arjun paused for a moment, thinking. His whole life had been about keeping his wealth a secret, but tonight, he didn't want to hide anymore. Maybe, just maybe, opening up would help him win real friends.

Arjun: *"Look, if you really want to know... come to my place this weekend. I'll show you everything."*

His friends stared at him in surprise.

Bhati: *"Your place, huh? Alright, we're in. But you better be ready for a lot of questions!"*

They laughed, and with the suite now ready, they entered the luxurious room, their excitement growing. The night unfolded into a mix of laughter, drinks, and stories. The general manager personally brought up the wine and steaks, adding a touch of elegance to their wild evening. Arjun, for the first time in a long while, felt like he was part of something again. Not just part of the college but part of a group of friends who finally accepted him for who he was, or at least who they were about to discover him to be.

As the night carried on, the suite buzzed with excitement and newfound camaraderie. Arjun looked around the room, watching Bhati, Naman, and Vicky joke around, and felt a flicker of hope. Maybe this new year wasn't going to be so lonely after all.

CHAPTER XIX

NEW FRIENDSHIPS AND REVELATIONS

Over the next few weeks, Arjun and Bhati grew closer as friends. Bhati, who once seemed like an enemy, now felt like a brother to Arjun. Their bond strengthened through small moments, shared lunches, late-night chats at the hostel, and long walks around the campus. Even Naman and Vicky, who had once mocked Arjun, now respected him deeply. The four of them had formed an unexpected but tight-knit group.

One day after class, Bhati and Arjun were sitting on the steps of H Block, talking about life and their future plans.

Bhati: *"You know, I never thought we'd become friends. Life is funny like that."*

Arjun: *"Yeah, sometimes the best friendships come from the most unexpected places."*

Bhati grinned, nudging Arjun's shoulder.

Bhati: *"It's good to have you around, man."*

That weekend, the long-awaited visit to Arjun's house finally arrived. Bhati, Naman, and Vicky were all excited, but nothing could have prepared them for what they were about to see. As soon as they entered Golf Links, Delhi, their jaws dropped. The grand mansion loomed ahead, surrounded by sprawling lawns, luxury cars parked in the driveway, and a vast entrance that resembled something straight out of a movie.

Bhati: *"This... this is your house?"*

Arjun: *"Yeah... welcome to my world."*

They stepped inside, and the interior was even more breathtaking. Expensive paintings adorned the walls, chandeliers hung from the ceilings, and the furniture was nothing short of regal. Arjun led them through the hallways, showing them around the house.

Vicky: *"I've never seen anything like this. Man, you've been living like this all along?"*

Arjun chuckled, a bit embarrassed by their awe.

Arjun: *"Yeah, I guess. But honestly, I don't show it because I don't want people to treat me differently. I just want to be known for who I am, not for my money."*

Naman's eyes widened as something clicked in his mind.

Naman: *"Wait... Arjun, is your father Karan?"*

Arjun nodded, and Naman's mouth dropped open even further.

Naman: *"Dude! My dad talks about your dad all the time! He's like his most important client. You're a really big personality in this city."*

Arjun smiled softly.

Arjun: *"Yeah, but that's exactly why I keep it quiet. I want to make real friends, people who don't care about my background."*

Bhati clapped him on the back.

Bhati: *"You've got that now, brother. We're here for you, no matter what."*

Arjun led them up to the terrace, where an even bigger surprise awaited. The group stood in awe as they saw a newly built helipad, sleek and modern, sitting on the rooftop.

Bhati: *"A helipad? Are you serious?"*

Arjun grinned.

Arjun: *"Yeah, I've got a little surprise for you. I earned my flying licence last month."*

He gestured towards the sleek helicopter sitting on the helipad.

Vicky: *"No way! You can fly that thing?"*

Arjun: *"Why don't I show you?"*

The excitement was palpable as they all climbed aboard. Arjun started the helicopter, and soon, they were lifting off, soaring above the city. The view was breathtaking as they hovered over India Gate and the sprawling streets of Delhi below them.

Naman: *"This is insane! I never thought I'd see the city from up here."*

Bhati: *"You've got some serious skills, Arjun."*

As they flew over Amity College, they looked down at the vast campus that had brought them together. For a moment, there was a sense of pride in all of them.

Vicky: *"You know, despite everything, we're part of something special. Amity has shaped us in ways we never expected."*

Bhati: *"Yeah. Say what you will about the college; it teaches you things you didn't even know you needed to learn."*

They all nodded in agreement, feeling a newfound sense of respect for their institution and the values it instilled in them.

After the exhilarating helicopter ride, they returned to Arjun's home for dinner. The table was set with a lavish spread of food, and they spent the evening talking, laughing, and enjoying each other's company.

Bhati: *"Thanks for today, man. I think we all needed this."*

Arjun: *"I'm glad you guys came. It feels good to finally share this part of my life with people I trust."*

As the night came to a close, the group felt closer than ever. Arjun, who had once felt so alone, now found himself surrounded by true friends. For the first time in a long while, he felt at peace. The bonds they had forged were real, built on trust, respect, and understanding. This was just the beginning of a new chapter, one filled with hope, excitement, and friendship.

CHAPTER XX

A GLIMMER OF THE PAST

Arjun's life had taken a positive turn. With Bhati, Naman, and Vicky by his side, college life was at its peak. The final year had electric energy, and everyone was aware that these carefree days would be over in just three short months. Classes were lighthearted, lunches were full of laughter, and the nights felt endless with parties, pranks, and deep conversations. Arjun finally felt like he was where he belonged.

Yet, amid the fun, there was one lingering thought in his mind: his relationship with Ishika. As he watched his friends joke around one afternoon, his mind wandered back to the moments they shared and the misunderstandings that had kept them apart.

That evening, he found himself sending a message to Ishika.

Arjun: *"Hey, Ishika. Can we talk? I feel like we never really cleared things up between us."*

It didn't take long for her to reply.

Ishika: *"Sure. Let's meet at the park near campus after dinner?"*

They met later that evening in the quiet park just off campus. The sun was setting, casting a warm orange glow over the trees. They walked slowly, not really knowing where to start.

Arjun: *"I've been thinking... about us. About what happened."*

Ishika glanced over at him, her expression soft but guarded.

Ishika: *"Yeah, me too. I think we both got caught up in the wrong things."*

Arjun sighed, relieved that they were finally talking about it.

Arjun: *"I wish we hadn't let all those misunderstandings pull us apart. We could have had something different."*

Ishika nodded, her gaze focused ahead as they walked.

Ishika: *"Maybe. But I've moved on now. It's not that simple anymore."*

Her words hit him harder than he expected, but there was no bitterness in her tone, just honesty. They continued their walk, talking about the past, about what went wrong, and about the people they had become. When it was time to part ways, there was a lingering silence between them.

Ishika: *"You know, Arjun, I've been thinking too. Maybe if things had gone differently... I don't know. We could have had a different story."*

She left him with those words, and as she walked away, Arjun couldn't help but wonder what could have been.

That night, Ishika sat in her room, thinking about their conversation. She hadn't expected to feel anything, but there was a nagging feeling in her heart. Could there still be something between them? The thought lingered as she went to bed, unsure of what the future held.

The next day in class, Ishika couldn't help but glance over at Arjun. He was laughing with his friends, completely unaware of her watchful eyes. She thought about their conversation the previous night. Maybe... just maybe, there was still something there.

As they filed out of class for lunch, Ishika found herself walking behind Arjun and his friends as they strolled through H Block. She couldn't resist any longer. She walked up to Arjun and tapped him on the shoulder.

Ishika: *"Hey, Arjun. Got a minute?"*

Arjun turned around, surprised to see her.

Arjun: *"Sure, what's up?"*

His friends gave them curious looks but soon drifted away, leaving the two of them standing there.

Ishika: *"I've been thinking about what we talked about last night. I know I said I moved on, but... maybe I haven't completely."*

Arjun looked at her, a flicker of something hopeful lighting up in his chest.

Arjun: *"What are you saying?"*

Ishika hesitated, a small smile playing on her lips.

Ishika: *"I'm saying... maybe we still have a chance. What do you think?"*

Arjun didn't know how to respond. There was no easy answer, but for the first time in a long while, it felt like there was a possibility; something was cooking up between them again.

Arjun stared at Ishika, her words hanging in the air between them. It felt like time had slowed down as he processed what she'd just said. Could they really have a second chance after all the misunderstandings, after everything that had come between them?

Arjun: *"Ishika, I... I don't know. Things have changed so much. I mean, I've changed. And you said you moved on."*

Ishika shrugged, looking a bit conflicted herself.

Ishika: *"I thought I had. But seeing you now, talking like we did last night, it made me realise that maybe I didn't completely let go."*

Arjun could see the uncertainty in her eyes. She wasn't just saying this casually; she was feeling its weight just as much as he was. The moments they shared, the good and the bad, were coming back to both of them.

They started walking again, slowly, as the other students around them laughed and chatted in the lively atmosphere of H Block. Neither of them said much for a few moments, just letting the noise of the campus fill the silence between them.

Arjun: *"Ishika, I've been thinking about you too. A lot, actually. After everything that happened, I've been wondering... if maybe I was wrong about some things. If maybe we didn't give it a real shot."*

Ishika smiled softly at that, glancing over at him.

Ishika: *"I guess we're both guilty of that. But maybe we needed this time apart to figure ourselves out. Now, we're different people than we were back then."*

Arjun nodded. She was right. They had both changed so much since the first year of college when their misunderstandings had created a rift between them. Arjun had grown more confident and had found himself in new friendships, and Ishika had matured, moving past the arrogance that had once defined her.

Arjun: *"So... where does that leave us?"*

They stopped walking, standing at the edge of the open courtyard where students milled about, enjoying their lunch breaks. Ishika turned to face him, her eyes searching his.

Ishika: *"I don't know, Arjun. I'm not saying everything is magically fixed. But maybe we can start fresh. See where things go."*

Arjun smiled, a small spark of hope igniting in his chest.

Arjun: *"I'd like that. A fresh start."*

They stood there for a moment, the tension between them dissolving into something lighter, something that felt hopeful, maybe even exciting. There was no need for a grand declaration or promises of what would happen next. Just the acknowledgement that something was still there, something worth exploring again.

The rest of the day felt different to both of them. During lunch, as Arjun and his friends wandered around H Block, he couldn't help but notice Ishika's gaze following him from across the courtyard. She was sitting with her friends, laughing and talking, but every now and then, their eyes would meet, and a shared smile would pass between them.

Bhati: *"What's going on between you and Ishika, man? I saw you two talking earlier."*

Arjun chuckled, shaking his head.

Arjun: *"Nothing... I mean, I don't know. We talked last night and cleared some things up. It feels like there might be something there again."*

Naman: *"Well, whatever it is, you're glowing, bro. Just take it slow."*

The others laughed, nudging Arjun playfully, but inside, he couldn't stop thinking about Ishika. Maybe there really was something still between them, something that had been waiting all this time to come back to life.

Later that afternoon, after classes, Arjun found himself walking alone through the campus gardens. He hadn't planned on running into Ishika again, but as fate would have it, she was there too, sitting on one of the benches, lost in thought. When she saw him, she smiled and waved him over.

Ishika: *"Hey. Funny seeing you here."*

Arjun: *"Yeah, I was just walking. Needed some fresh air."*

He sat down beside her, and for a moment, they just enjoyed the quiet of the gardens. The air was cool, the sun beginning to dip below the horizon.

Ishika: *"I've been thinking about us again... after today."*

Arjun looked over at her, curious.

Arjun: *"And?"*

Ishika leaned back against the bench, sighing softly.

Ishika: *"And I think... maybe we shouldn't overthink it. If there's something between us, we'll figure it out. If not, at least we'll know."*

Arjun nodded, feeling the same way. There was no need to rush or to force anything. What would happen would happen naturally.

Arjun: *"You're right. Let's just see what happens."*

They sat there for a while longer, not needing to say much. There was a quiet understanding between them now, a mutual respect and an acknowledgement of their shared history. The past was still there, but maybe, just maybe, the future held something different for them.

As the sun set behind the trees, they stood up and walked back towards campus together, side by side. It wasn't clear what would come next, but for now, they were content with the possibility of a new beginning.

CHAPTER XXI

UNWRITTEN CHAPTERS

It was an unexpectedly free period. Ankita Ma'am had taken leave for the day, and the moment word got around, excitement buzzed through the classroom. With no professor in sight, the students quickly began to relax, some pulling out snacks, others chatting animatedly.

Outside, rain drizzled softly against the windows, creating a soothing backdrop to the lively atmosphere inside. Arjun, Bhati, Naman, Vicky, Ishika, and the rest of the gang gathered around in a loose circle of desks, making the most of the rare break in their busy schedule. The atmosphere was lighthearted, filled with the sounds of laughter, the casual hum of conversation, and the rhythmic patter of rain.

Naman: *"A free period! Feels like we're back in first year, doesn't it?"*

Vicky: *"Man, I remember those days. We'd spend every break exploring campus, finding new spots to hang out."*

Ishika: *"Right? Remember how we used to chill by the bookstore in H Block? Those were the days."*

There was a collective sigh as everyone seemed to drift into nostalgic memories. It was the final year, and the weight of everything coming to an end within just a few months hung in the air.

Arjun: *"You know, I never realised how much I'd miss this place. When we first came here, I thought it was just another college, but now..."* He smiled. *"It's like a second home."*

Bhati: *"Exactly. I mean, where else would we find a place with this kind of vibe? The campus is massive, but somehow, it's so easy to feel like you belong here."*

Vidhi: *"Not to mention, Amity just has this way of pushing you to do better. Look at us! We've all changed so much since first year."*

Naomi chimed in with a grin. *"Yeah, remember how lost we all were on the first day? Wandering around trying to find F Block? It feels like forever ago."*

The group laughed, recalling their awkward first steps into college life, unsure of everything and everyone.

Marban: *"The thing about Amity is, it doesn't just give you academics. It gives you an experience. All those events, clubs, fests... They're what made this place special."*

Ananya: *"Sangathan... what a ride that was. I'll never forget how intense that competition was. But it brought us all closer, didn't it?"*

Arjun nodded, remembering the pride he felt when his team fought hard during the competitions.

Arjun: *"It's not just the big moments, though. It's the little things, like hanging out at the cafes, chilling on the porch by the hostel, and even those late-night study sessions in the library."*

Ishika: *"Or the fact that every corner of this place has a memory attached to it. Even H Block, it's not just a building. It's where we spent most of our time, making memories we'll never forget."*

There was a moment of quiet reflection as everyone took in the truth of her words. Amity College had become more than just a place to study; it was where friendships were formed, where they grew as people, and where they had some of the best moments of their lives.

Bhati: *"You know what I'll miss the most? The fact that we could be anyone we wanted to be here. We all came from different places with different backgrounds, but somehow, we found a way to connect. That's the magic of this place."*

Vidhi: *"It's true. We came here as strangers, but we're leaving as something more. We're leaving as a family."*

Vicky: *"And no matter where life takes us after this, Amity will always be a part of who we are."*

The group nodded in agreement, their smiles tinged with the bittersweet realisation that these moments were fleeting. But for now, they still had time; time to enjoy the final stretch of their college days, time to appreciate everything Amity had given them.

As the bell rang, signalling the end of the free period, they stood up, stretching and gathering their things. There was a lightness in the air, and though the future awaited them just around the corner, for now, they could still hold onto these moments.

Arjun: *"You know, we should make the most of these last few months. Really savour everything. These days won't come again."*

Ishika smiled a glint of nostalgia in her eyes. *"You're right, Arjun. Let's make every moment count."*

And with that, they headed out of the classroom, knowing that these final months at Amity would be filled with more laughter, more memories, and a bond that would stay with them long after they walked out of those gates for the last time.

After the free period ended, Arjun and Ishika found themselves gravitating towards each other, a natural pull that neither could ignore. They casually walked through the campus, their conversation light and easy. Soon, they found themselves heading toward I Block, which was quieter than usual due to the MBA students being on break.

The corridors were empty, and a peaceful stillness surrounded them as they wandered through the isolated halls. Arjun and Ishika exchanged knowing glances, their unspoken connection hanging between them. As they walked, they came across an empty classroom.

Ishika: *"Want to check it out? I haven't been in this block in ages."*

Arjun smiled, following her inside. The room was empty, the silence giving it an almost serene feeling. They sat on the benches, continuing their conversation, their laughter filling the space.

But soon, the air between them shifted. Their laughter faded, and they found themselves lost in each other's eyes, the memories of their past encounters resurfacing. That kiss from before—the one neither of them could forget—lingered in both their minds.

Ishika: *"Remember... last time we were alone like this?"*

Arjun didn't need to answer. The memory was as vivid for him as it was for her. Without thinking, the pull between them grew stronger. He leaned in, his breath catching slightly, and before either of them knew it, their lips met again in a passionate kiss.

The intensity of the moment took over. Their kiss deepened, their hands exploring each other's faces and shoulders, the energy between them electric. They laid back on the bench, the closeness between them making it impossible to think of anything else but the connection they shared.

For a few moments, the world outside disappeared, and it was just the two of them, wrapped in each other's warmth. The kiss intensified, filled with longing and the unspoken feelings they had carried for so long. They didn't need words to express what was happening–they simply felt it, moving together in a rhythm that was both new and familiar.

But just as the moment threatened to pull them completely into one another, the door creaked open, startling them both. They quickly sat up, their hearts racing, only to see the cleaning staff standing awkwardly at the door, clearly as surprised as they were.

Cleaning Staff: *"Oh... sorry... I'll... I'll come back later."*

There was an awkward pause as the staff quickly exited, closing the door behind them. Arjun and Ishika looked at each other wide-eyed for a moment, and then they both burst into laughter. The tension melted into something lighter, and the embarrassment of the situation only added to the connection they had just shared.

Ishika: *"Well, that was... something."*

Arjun: *"Yeah, definitely not what I was expecting today."*

They both stood up, still laughing, the intensity of the previous moments easing into something playful and light. They glanced at each other with a spark of mischief in their eyes.

Ishika: *"You're trouble, you know that?"*

Arjun: *"Takes one to know one."*

They walked out of the classroom, still grinning, their hearts lighter despite the interrupted moment. The connection between them was undeniable now, and though they weren't sure where things would go from here, they both felt a sense of excitement and curiosity about what the future might hold.

For now, though, they were content with the playful glances and the thrill of what had just happened, their bond stronger than ever before.

CHAPTER XXII

THE UNSPOKEN FAREWELL

The announcement of the farewell party spread through the campus like wildfire, stirring a mix of emotions among the students. It was the culmination of years spent together, a final celebration before everyone would scatter to chase their own destinies. For Arjun and his friends, the impending end of their college days brought an equal measure of excitement and melancholy. The familiar halls of Amity, once buzzing with the energy of youth and endless possibilities, now seemed tinged with a bittersweet nostalgia.

As preparations for the event began, the campus transformed. Decorations appeared almost overnight: glittering lights strung between trees, colourful banners draped over railings, and a stage set up in the main courtyard where students would gather for performances. The air was thick with anticipation, the kind that only comes when you know something significant is about to happen, something that will be remembered for years to come.

It was a rainy week, the kind that brings both gloom and a sense of renewal. The soft patter of rain against the windows became a constant companion, mirroring the emotional undercurrent running through the students. Arjun often found himself staring out at the rain, lost in thought. The reality of the approaching farewell weighed heavily on his mind, not just because of the end of an era but because of the unresolved feelings he harboured for Ishika.

Their relationship had blossomed over the past few months. What started as tension and misunderstanding slowly evolved into something deeper. They had shared countless moments, late-night conversations, quiet walks around the campus, and stolen kisses that left them both breathless. Yet, despite the closeness, one thing remained unsaid between them: *I love you.* The words lingered in Arjun's mind, heavy with meaning, but every time he thought about saying them, something held him back.

The day of the farewell party arrived, and the campus was transformed into a dazzling scene of beauty and celebration. The rain had stopped, leaving the air fresh and cool, with the lingering scent of wet earth and blooming flowers. Students dressed in their finest outfits, the girls in elegant dresses and the boys in sharp suits, each trying to outdo the other. The atmosphere was electric, filled with excitement, laughter, and the bittersweet knowledge that this was their last night together as students.

Arjun felt a mix of emotions as he walked across the campus, the familiar paths now adorned with lights and decorations. His mind kept drifting to Ishika, who was busy with her final preparations for the dance performance. He knew tonight would be his last chance to tell her how he felt. The thought both thrilled and terrified him.

As he entered the main courtyard, the sound of music filled the air, and the sight of his friends laughing and enjoying themselves brought a smile to his face. Bhati, Naman, Vicky, and the rest of the gang were all there, their usual banter masking the underlying sadness of the occasion. Despite the emotional weight of the evening, the atmosphere was lively and full of energy.

Naman: *"Can you believe this is it? Our last party as students?"*

Bhati: *"I know, man. It feels surreal. Amity really pulled out all the stops for this one."*

Vicky: *"Look at this place! They've turned the campus into a fairy tale. Even the rain couldn't stop the magic tonight."*

Arjun smiled at his friend's excitement, but his thoughts were elsewhere. The words he wanted to say to Ishika weighed heavily on his mind. He kept scanning the crowd, looking for her, his heart pounding with anticipation and fear.

The lights dimmed as the programme began, and the students gathered around the stage. The farewell speeches were delivered, full of fond memories and well wishes, but Arjun barely heard them. His thoughts were consumed by the impending moment, the words he had been holding back for so long. As Ishika took the stage, the world seemed to slow down. She looked stunning, her dress shimmering under the lights, her movements fluid and captivating.

Arjun watched, his heart swelling with admiration and love. Every step she took on that stage was a reminder of why he had fallen for her. Memories of their time together flashed through his mind, their first awkward encounter, the arguments, the laughter, and the quiet moments that had meant so much. *After her performance,* he told himself, *I'll tell her after the performance.*

The music swelled, and Ishika danced with a passion that left the audience spellbound. Arjun couldn't take his eyes off her; every move was a reminder of what he had come to cherish so deeply. But as the final notes played and her performance came to an end, reality came crashing down.

As the applause filled the courtyard, Ishika walked over to Arjun, her face a mixture of emotions. She was beautiful, yes, but there was a sadness in her eyes that made Arjun's heart skip a beat.

Ishika: *"Arjun, I need to talk to you."*

His heart raced. *This is it,* he thought. *This is the moment.* But her next words hit him like a cold wave.

Ishika: *"I'm moving to the USA after college. My family and I are leaving right after graduation."*

Arjun felt the ground shift beneath him. He had been so focused on what he wanted to say that he hadn't considered the possibility that she might leave. The words he had been preparing—*I love you*—suddenly seemed futile. His mouth went dry, and for a moment, he was lost for words.

Arjun: *"I... I didn't know."*

Ishika smiled softly, a sad, almost resigned expression on her face.

Ishika: *"I just found out recently. It's going to be a big change, but... well, that's life, right?"*

Arjun nodded, swallowing the lump in his throat. The moment he had been waiting for was slipping away, and there was nothing he could do to stop it. He thought about all the moments they had shared, and he realised that maybe some things were not meant to last forever, no matter how much you wanted them to.

Arjun: *"Yeah... maybe some things are just meant to be temporary."*

They exchanged a bittersweet smile, a silent understanding passing between them. The words they had left unsaid seemed to hang in the air, but neither of them needed to say more. Their time together had been beautiful, but it was now coming to an end.

As the night wore on, Arjun found himself surrounded by his friends, trying to push the pain aside. Bhati, Naman, Vicky, and the others were in high spirits, determined to make the most of their final night together.

Bhati: *"There he is! Where did you disappear to, lover boy?"*

Vicky: *"Probably getting all sentimental, huh?"* (laughs)

Naman: *"Can you blame him? This is our last night together, after all."*

Arjun forced a smile, trying to shake off the lingering sadness. *I can't dwell on it now,* he thought. *This is our last night—let's make it count.*

Arjun: *"Yeah, just needed a minute. But I'm here now. Let's make the most of it."*

Bhati: *"That's the spirit! Come on, let's hit the dance floor one last time!"*

They headed to the dance floor, where the music was loud, and the energy was high. Despite the fun, Arjun's mind kept drifting back to Ishika, replaying their conversation in his head.

Vicky (noticing Arjun's distraction): *"You okay, bro?"*

Arjun (sighs): *"Yeah, just thinking about how fast time flies. It's hard to believe this is it."*

Bhati: *"We'll stay in touch, man. This isn't the end, just the beginning of a new chapter."*

Naman: *"Exactly. We've got memories that'll last a lifetime. And who knows what the future holds?"*

Arjun nodded, appreciating their words but still feeling the weight of what he hadn't been able to say. He tried to focus on the present, on the laughter and the music, on the friends who had become like family.

As the night wound down, the group gathered outside, looking out over the campus, now bathed in the soft glow of the party lights.

Vicky: *"This place... it's been home for so long. Feels weird to say goodbye."*

Bhati: *"It's not goodbye, just see you later."*

Arjun stood silently, looking at the campus that had been their world for so long. There was something magical about that night, a sense of closure, of knowing that no matter what happened next, they had lived through something special.

Arjun (to himself): *"Maybe not everything lasts forever... but some moments will always stay with you."*

His friends turned to him, questioning looks on their faces.

Naman: *"What was that, Arjun?"*

Arjun smiled, a mix of sadness and contentment settling in his heart.

Arjun: *"Nothing. Just thinking about how lucky we are to have had this time together."*

Bhati: *"Damn right. Now, come on, let's make the most of these last few hours!"*

With that, they headed back into the party, ready to enjoy the final moments of an unforgettable farewell. And for those few hours, Arjun let himself be fully present, cherishing the laughter, the music, and the memories that would last a lifetime.

CHAPTER XXIII

A LETTER TO ANUSHKA

Dear Anushka,

It's been a while since you left for Dubai, and I've been meaning to write to you. I guess now is the right time, especially with everything that has happened here on campus. A lot has changed since you left, and I find myself looking back at it all: our time together, the people we've met, and the moments that shaped us.

I'm not sure where to begin, so I'll just start with the biggest thing on my mind: Ishika. You know how we were always so close, yet there were always things left unsaid? Well, those things never quite made it to the surface. We spent so much time together, and there was a moment when I thought that maybe, just maybe, we were more than friends. But, Anushka, I never said it. I never told her that I loved her.

There were so many times I wanted to say it. You know how bad I am with timing, right? I'd catch her eye during one of our conversations or after one of our kisses, and I'd feel it in my chest, those words I was holding back. But I guess I was always waiting for the perfect moment. I thought maybe at the farewell, I'd finally confess.

But life has a funny way of shifting things when you least expect it. After her performance at the farewell, I was all set to tell her how I felt. And then, just like that, she told me she was moving to the USA with her family. Before I could even say anything, she was already moving on to a new chapter, and there I was, left with the words still stuck in my throat.

It hit me hard. I kept thinking, *What if I'd just said it sooner? Would things have been different?* But after reflecting on it, I realised something. Whatever Ishika and I shared was beautiful in its own way. Maybe we didn't need the words. Maybe it wasn't meant to be a grand love story. What we had was special, and it made my time at Amity unforgettable. But maybe it was just that–a chapter in the story of our lives, not the whole book.

I can't say I'm not a little sad that we never got that chance to see what we could have been. But I'm also happy, Anushka. Happy that I got to experience those moments with her, with you, with Yash, with Bhati and the others. I wouldn't trade any of it for anything. Not the laughter, not the late-night talks, not the pranks, not the incredible farewells. And especially not the bonds we built.

I still think about you all the time. You were right; by the way, these moments are fleeting, but they leave a mark. Our time at Amity is over, but the experiences, the friendships, and the laughter stay with us. It's funny, isn't it? How a place can mean so much, how the people we meet in those hallways can shape us in ways we don't even realise at the time.

I've come to understand that not everything needs to be eternal to be meaningful. Some relationships, some moments, they're beautiful because they're temporary. They're like shooting stars; you catch them for a moment, and then they're gone, but they leave behind something magical.

So, I guess that's where I am now. Happy. Content. And grateful for everything we've been through. There's no regret in my heart, only appreciation. Ishika and I may have had something fleeting, but it was ours, and it was perfect in its own way.

I miss you, Anushka. I hope Dubai is treating you well. I'll be visiting soon, and we'll catch up properly. There's still so much to tell you, so much to laugh about. But for now, I just wanted to share this with you. It feels like the closing of a chapter, but as with all good stories, it leaves room for new beginnings.

Take care of yourself, and keep shining, just like you always do.

With love,
Arjun

And with that, Arjun folded the letter, feeling a sense of closure wash over him. The story of his college life at Amity had come to an end, but it was a story he would carry with him forever. There were no loose ends, only fond memories and the knowledge that, sometimes, the most beautiful things are the ones that leave us a little too soon.

The future awaited him, full of possibilities, and he was ready to embrace it, grateful for the past and open to whatever came next.

Feedback Questions

These questions are designed in a manner to help the writer understand what the readers think about the story and characters. Please answer these questions only after reading the whole story. You can mail the answers along with any other feedback to mayankgupta7c@gmail.com.

1. Arjun's decision to conceal his wealth was a pivotal part of his character. Did this make him more admirable in your eyes, or did it create a barrier between you and his true self? How did this secret shape your perception of his integrity?

2. Ishika chose to leave for the USA without fully considering the impact on her relationship with Arjun. Did this decision make you empathise with her situation, or did it make you question her commitment and emotional depth? How did this choice affect your connection to her character?

3. Bhati's shift from being a bully to showing signs of redemption is central to his arc. Did you find his transformation believable, or did it feel forced? Were you left convinced of his growth, or did you feel he was just a product of his circumstances?

4. Anushka played a crucial role as Arjun's confidante. Did you find her advice empowering for him, or did you feel she sometimes held him back from making his own choices? Were there moments when you questioned whether her influence was truly beneficial to his journey?

5. Naman and Vicky stood by Bhati through thick and thin.

Did their loyalty strike you as admirable, or did it make you question their moral compass? How did their unwavering support impact your view of their characters and their role in the story?

Disclaimer

This book is a work of fiction. Names, characters, places, and events are the product of the author's imagination or are used fictitiously. Any resemblance to actual persons, living or dead, events, or locales is entirely coincidental.

The author has made every effort to ensure that the content of this book is accurate and reflective of the setting and situations described. However, the narrative and dialogue are artistic interpretations and should not be taken as a factual representation of any institution or individual.

The author wants to expressly make it clear that it is not his story. All characters are fictional, though they might endure a few characteristics of the people known to the author.

The views and opinions expressed in this book are those of the characters and do not necessarily reflect the views or opinions of any real organisations, institutions, or the author.

About The Author

Mayank Gupta is a master of storytelling and a graduate of Amity University, where he earned his master's degree in law. His time at Amity not only shaped his professional career but also inspired him to explore the intricate dynamics of relationships, ambition, and self-discovery that he brings to life in his writing. His debut novel, **'Appearances'**, is a reflection of his deep understanding of the complexities of human emotions, set against the glamorous yet deceptive backdrop of college life.

Having experienced the vibrant campus culture firsthand, Mayank blends his personal insights with compelling narratives, offering readers a unique perspective on the fine line between what we project to the world and what we keep hidden beneath the surface. One can expect lots of turns of events during the story, with sudden incidents that reshape the entire narrative and bring interesting twists to the story.

When not writing, Mayank enjoys travelling, exploring new ideas for stories, or engaging with creative projects. He is passionate about sharing stories that resonate on a deeply emotional level, inspired by his life experiences.